CRIME AND CONSCIENCE

By

DN Miller

Copyright © 2023 by DN Miller

All rights reserved.

No part of this book may be reproduced, stored in a retrieval system or transmitted in any form or by any means without the prior written permission of the publishers, except by a reviewer who may quote brief passages in a review to be printed in a newspaper, magazine or journal.

The final approval for this literary material is granted by the author.

PART I

Chapter I

"Don't judge each day by the harvest you reap, but by the seeds that you plant."

Crime and Conscience

She walked with confidence as she reassured herself, repeating several times in her head, "I've got this. I've got this." Her six inch Gucci heels clicked clacked along the pavement, while her thick hips and firm ass bounced from side to side. Wearing an all-black suit with a pop of color always seemed to land her the job. That was her go to suit. You know the one that kisses every inch of your curves, revealing everything but showing nothing and still managing to look professional; yes, that one. She always believed women had an advantage over men. No matter if a man is married or not, men will always want what they can't have; in the bedroom or on the job.

She got stares from the women and men. Mostly the women, they were always jealous of Tajh. They were always trying to figure out her deal. Was she Black; was she White; was she mixed? Most women thought she was a white woman trying to be black. Tajh always got categorized, but she was just her. Her dirty blonde dreads that she always wore in a bun confused everyone and her having green eyes didn't make it any better. She stood out; less because of her appearance and more because of her ego. What Tajh want's, Tajh always gets.

She grew up in the foster care system, bouncing from house to house. No one ever really knew what her race was, including her. She got into a lot of fights, trying to always prove she wasn't a punk. She always got tested. Tajh always kept a book in her hand. Being a loner, books always helped her escape reality. She spent most of her teen years in Detroit, finally finding a family who she could vibe with. She ran away from the last three foster families. There was always either the dad or a foster brother who tried to fuck her. In one incident, they tried to double team her; the foster mom walked in on it. Police found her on the side of the road, passed out. Child protective service had been looking for her for a month. They ended up placing her with a family in Detroit.

Tajh moved to San Antonio Texas with her foster parents' aunt. She wanted a new start. She'd always had this vision and a drive for success. She didn't know how she was going to do it, but knew she needed to make a move if anything was going to happen.

"Hello, I'm here to register for the real estate event." Tajh stood at the registration table waiting for her folder and name tag. She took her last three hundred dollars to pay for this event, hoping it would give her the tools she needed to be financially free—at least, that's what they advertised.

"Just go right through those double doors and sit anywhere."

"Thank you." Tajh grabbed her name tag, peeled the back off, and pasted it over her suit jacket, just below her collar. There were at least a thousand people there. She started trying to add up the numbers in her head on how much this convention made off these people. One hundred dollars a person and VIP was three hundred dollars. These real estate guru's were making bank off them and she wanted to be a part of it.

She admired everyone as she walked through the doors. She'd never been in a setting with so many people, mostly Black at that, unless it was in a courtroom. It was very loud from all the multiple conversations going on. The 44,000 square feet convention center was filled with people eager to change their finances. "Hello everyone, thank you for being here with us this weekend, here at the lovely Harlingen in San Antonio Texas!" He went on to introduce himself, "I am Jonathan Smith, real estate guru. I started out just like you!" Tajh pulled out her notebook and began writing down key points Mr.

Smith was touching base on as he delivered his speech. He had the crowd amped up. She was excited and couldn't wait to absorb all the information that he was giving.

"Is this seat taken?" someone asked. His heavy accent led her to believe he was from an island.

Still writing in her note book and not paying any attention to him, she answered, "No, it isn't, help yourself." He sat right next to her. She was in deep thought, trying to make sure she wrote down everything the real estate guru was saying.

"Is this your first time coming to one of these?"

Tajh looked up to answer him but stuttered when she began to talk. He was gorgeous. His perfectly white teeth highlighted his smile. His dark black chocolate skin glowed through the dull lighting of the conference room. His blue-black messy dreads were pulled up into a ponytail with a couple sticking out, almost like a messy bun that the White girls love wearing. He was not the typical guy that would normally catch her eye. The flashy type, who didn't mind spending money on her just for a little bit of her attention. You could spot these suckas a mile away. Attention whores begging for bragging rights, but secretly paying.

He held out his hand. "Hello, I'm Khori."

Tajh smiled, trying to avoid eye contact. "Hello, I'm Tajh."

He repeated himself, "Is this your first time attending one of these?"

"Yes, it is."

He had on a dark blue long sleeve button down shirt with tiny peach flamingos scattered on it. The two top buttons were unbuttoned and an 18 kt yellow gold BVLGARI pendant necklace was draped around his neck with a brass key. He reminded her of Puff Daddy—casually dressed but looking elegant. She sized him up as the two carried on a conversation. He wore dark blue dress slacks with matching peach dress socks and some slides on black loafers. His pants fit him so well that Tajh could clearly see an imprint of his Dick. He looked well off, appeared single, had no ring on or no marks around his ring finger indicating he was married. Still, men like him are too good to be true. They can be the right catch but for the wrong fisher men. Nowadays, people aren't honest and won't tell you their sexual preference.

"Is this your first time coming to one?" He looked like he had a little bit of money, Tajh wanted to know what his hustle was without asking him.

"No, I come to these conventions often," he replied, smiling.

"How often is that?"

"Twice a year, they pick different locations..."

Tajh continued to listen to Mr. Smith as he introduced the next guest speaker.

Twelve o'clock came and it was lunch time. The committee informed everyone to be back at one. She grabbed her notebook and proceeded to get up off her chair. "Where are you going for lunch?"

"Excuse me?"

He asked her again, "I said; where are you going for lunch?"

Tajh really didn't have a place to go for lunch. In fact, she didn't have any money. "I was under the impression lunch was provided for us, but I see it isn't. I didn't bring my credit cards. So, nowhere." She knew how to ask for what she wanted without giving details. This separated the giving men from broke men.

"Well, if you'd like to join me for lunch, I got you. You can treat me next time."

She didn't respond right away, giving a second before she answered him. Tajh didn't want to seem too eager. "Sure, that's fine." She thought to herself, *This cocky muthafucka, how does he know if there's gonna be a next time?*

She grabbed her notebook and proceeded to get up. "I'll get that for you." He escorted her through the entrance to the main lobby. A sign of a true gentleman or just a little game. The two were side by side as he put the palm of his right hand on her lower back, leading her through the main doors. Being that she dated all sorts of men, only rich White men did that.

Who is this man and where did he learn this gesture from? she thought.

He pulled out his ticket and gave it to the valet attendant. "Do you have a place in mind for lunch?"

"It depends, what are you in the mood for?"

"I could eat a nice chicken salad."

"Chicken salad it is then."

Most men would have chosen steak, but from the size of his physique, she could tell he was into himself, working out and drinking lots of water. His skin was so smooth, not even a raiser bump. His black Benz pulled up and the valet attendant got out and handed him his keys. She stood there waiting to see if he was going to open the door for her. "Oh, I don't do that."

"Do what?"

"Open doors for women." Tajh rolled her eyes, giving him this 'dude you better open this damn door,' stare. He giggled, "I'm just playing."

"Ha ha, real funny. I see you've got a sense of humor."

He opened the passenger door and the aroma of weed lingered. It wasn't the blatant bold smell as if it was being smoked, but that raw subtle scent of it being fresh. His car was clean, not a stain or a smudge on site. She got in and he shut the door behind her. Her eyes landed on him as he walked over to the valet and tipped him twenty dollars, discreetly exchanging the money for a hand shake. He walked back to the car and got in. "So, where in Texas can a man eat a great salad?"

She turned towards him. "What, you're not from around here?"

"Let me guess, my accent gave it away."

The two chuckled. "Meaning, do you live in Texas? You said you go to these things all the time."

"Yes, I do go to these things all the time, and no, I do not live in Texas. In fact, I still live in Jamaica."

"You come all the way over here just to learn how to wholesale houses? Don't they offer that over there?"

Tajh's curiosity had Khori stumbling for words. "You sure do ask a lot of questions."

"Well, I need to know who I'm riding with. You could be into human trafficking or something."

"Do I look like I'm into killing people?"

"No, but neither did Ted Bundy."

"Comparing me to Ted Bundy, oh, I see."

"Hey, you never know. People are crazy as hell nowadays, especially in Texas."

Tajh continued to give Khori directions to the restaurant, "It's over there, make a left." She pointed to a small diner called Jason's Deli on the Sunshine Strip, a popular place in San Antonio mostly known for their salads. Lunch time always has this place packed. Cars took up nearly all the parking spots. "There's a spot right over there," Tajh pointed at the very end next to a small black car.

Tajh waited to get out to see if he was still going to be a gentleman and open her door. Most men only put on this act for a little bit before they start showing who they really are. He got out and walked around the front of the car and opened her door. "Thank you."

"You're welcome." He hurried up and got in front of her to open the door to the Deli. Tajh could tell he had a hidden agenda. But what? Did he want to sleep with her? It wasn't often that she met a man that was sexy, had his own money, and was generous without wanting something in return.

The two found a table in the back of the diner. The place was small and only had about ten tables. That was the only table that wasn't filled. The diner was set up with ten small wooden square high tables and two high chairs on each side. There was a buffet style salad bar at the very front of the diner, facing the front window, the only window. A counter with the cooks and waitresses was in the middle of the floor. You only went to the counter if you were ordering food to go.

"Hello, are you guys ready to order?" a short, blonde-haired woman asked. She was wearing a black apron and a faded black T-shirt. She looked like she was at least fifty years old. Probably been working there for a while—her slip resistant shoes were worn down and the tread on the bottom was uneven, forcing her to stand odd. There were food stains on her black slacks as if she was the cook and not the actual waitress.

"Yes, I'll have Amy's Turkey O with chips and an iced tea, please."

"And for you, sir?"

"I'll have the Nutty Mixed Up Salad and bottled water, please and thank you."

"OK, what type of dressing would you like?"

"Do you have French?"

"Yes, we do."

"I'll take French then."

"OK, I'll be right back with your drinks."

"Thank you."

Tajh pulled out her phone and began looking through Facebook. The awkward silence made her feel uncomfortable just sitting there. "Here's your drinks, it will be a minute for your food, we are a little short staffed today and today is usually one of our busiest days. So I apologize in advance."

"Thank you… So, were you born and raised here, Tajh?"

Setting her phone down on the table, she took a sip of her tea, eyeing him. "No, I wasn't."

"So, where are you from?"

"Why?"

"I'm just trying to make conversation, no hard feelings." Tajh had always been very careful who she told her business to. She didn't trust anyone. Being that she'd just met him, she wasn't about to just tell her whole life story. "OK, if you don't feel comfortable telling me that, then what brought you to Texas?" The food came and the waitress sat both of their plates in front of them before asking if they needed anything else. "So, Ms. Tajh, what brought you here?" Khori asked again when the waitress had left their table.

She picked up a chip, biting into it as she thought, *Does this man ever quit?* "Well, I had a bad break up. A year ago to be exact. I was happy until I met him. I was able to travel out of the country, eat exotic foods and explore places I never even heard of. I didn't have a trouble in the world. I didn't have any kids and didn't want any. The lifestyle that I was accustomed to, didn't allow me to have any room for anyone else, especially kids. I had rules when it came to dating. I didn't date men with children. You could say I was a bit selfish. I didn't like sharing my time with no one. I wanted to always be his first priority. My ex had kids. I didn't find out until a year later when I was already in love. I always found myself fighting for his time. He had four daughters. Them little heffa's was always in his pockets. Every time they called, he went running; not that I don't appreciate a man who takes care of his kids. But these little girls were being trained early to depend on men. I didn't stand a chance. Then the drama from his daughters' moms just made me want to leave the whole family alone. They always needed something; 'Kevin, can you take me shopping?' 'Kevin, can you fix this?' 'Kevin, I need, I need.' The shit was sickening—like they couldn't do most of these things on their own. They were so dependent on him; I couldn't wait to leave him. I ended up moving down here with my great aunt. She has a three bedroom house with nobody helping her. Her husband passed away and all her children moved out. I felt like this would be a great time to start over. I'd finally gotten over this man and decided to live my life. When I got here, I didn't know what my next move was going to be. All I knew was that I needed a job. I tried for weeks to get one but no one would hire me. I was either overqualified or didn't meet the requirements. I was getting desperate and my little thousand dollars was slowly depleting. I saw an ad posted on a billboard. A company teaching wholesale; they promised that if you invested in them, they would invest in you. I thought, 'What the hell, my pride isn't too big for this.' So, I spent my last three hundred dollars to see If I could become rich like they said." She made up the story so she could see where his head was at.

Munching down on her chips, she wondered if she'd made the right move by telling this total stranger her story. This made her want to know about him. "Okay, I know you're here for the wholesale event, obviously for money, but what's your story? Where are you from?"

Stuffing his face with salad, Khori couldn't wait to tell Tajh about his upbeat life. He produced this enormous smile while chewing on his food. "Well, I was born in Negril, Jamaica. My mother raised me and my older sister. My dad and my mother split up when I was very young. I never really knew my dad. We grew up poor but my mother always made a way for us. She is a Jewelry maker back home. That's how she's always made a living, making the most beautiful necklaces and earrings. She would mostly go to our marketplace and sell them. Sometimes, she would even barter, trading her pieces for food, clothes, and even shelter. It wasn't much, but we survived. I didn't like the way we grew up. I always promised my family that I would make it big someday so they wouldn't have to live poor."

"So, what did you do to change that? What brought you here?"

"You can say fate brought me here. A group of Americans came to our little town wanting to help. They wanted to learn about our culture. In exchange, I asked them to teach me business. We couldn't afford cell phones, so they helped me market my mother's jewelry on different platforms. I would split the money with my mom. The Americans started coming back a lot, bringing different people. I also earned money by taking them around Jamaica, being their tour guide. I saved up all my money, got a passport, and came to the US with the Americans. They ran this organization that housed me and helped me get a job. I didn't like working for other people. I was so used to working for myself—it didn't make sense to make someone else rich—so I took the skills my mother taught me and started making my own jewelry."

"But how did you get into selling houses?"

"About two years ago, I was renting a house off this lady, who was very sick. She told me she was going to sell the house because she couldn't keep up with it. I wanted it but I didn't have the money she was asking for. I had heard about different ways to get property without using your own money. I did a lot of research, watched a lot of videos, and then it hit me. I asked her if I could pay her monthly, give her a down payment of fifteen hundred and pay her four hundred a month and she agreed. So I put up a for rent sign. A couple people came to check out the house. I charged nine hundred for rent and security deposit. That's eighteen hundred dollars. I gave the old lady fifteen hundred and kept the remaining balance for myself. So, every month, they paid me nine hundred and I gave her four until my debt was paid off. She sold the house to me for twelve thousand, my contract was for thirty months. I figured, if I can find people who don't want their property, I can make a killing doing this. I started going to these conventions, learning different ways to buy and sell properties without using any of my money."

Tajh couldn't believe it; she was thirsty for his knowledge. He actually did it, coming from nothing like she did. A real life success story. She wanted to know more without looking desperate. They sat talking about real estate and money, and one o'clock came and went. "Oh my God! We're late." They both took the last sip of their drinks and signaled for the waitress to come with the check. Khori pulled out a black card. Tajh studied his movements and watched to see if he was going to leave a tip. She couldn't help but to think, *This man has money*. She didn't want his though. She wanted her own. She knew she needed him on her team if she was going to make this wholesaling gig work. He seemed like he definitely reaped the benefits and she wanted parts of it. The two gathered the remains of their food and headed out the door.

By the time the two got back to the convention center, they could see crowds of people exiting the building. Pulling up to the valet, Khori rolled down his window and asked the attendant if the convention was over. "Yes, it will resume tomorrow at 7.a.m."

He thanked the man and pulled off. "So, Tajh, we can do one of two things: I can drop you off at home or we can continue our own convention and you let me teach you a thing or two."

She saw this as her opportunity to learn first-hand about the business. Trusting her gut feeling, she decided to take Khori up on his offer. "I think I can kick it with you for a little while, but I need to get out of these clothes, my feet are killing me."

"First rule, always dress comfortably."

They drove about ten miles before reaching her aunt's house. As she unfastened her seat belt, grabbing her notebook, he got out, ran around to the passenger side and opened her door. "My lady." He bowed his head down, shutting the door behind her.

"Wait right here, I'll be back." She strutted up the five stone steps leading to her aunt's door. Being careful she didn't send the wrong signals, she bent down using her knees, making sure her ass remained facing in a downward position to get the spare key under a welcome mat. As soon as she went into the house, she instantly kicked off her stilettos and sat down on the chaise that was placed up against the wall by the entrance steps. Her aunt had one of those big old brick houses but everything inside was wood. It was so big, it looked like one of those plantation houses. Dark oak wood shutters surrounded every window. She even had an old cast iron bathtub shaped like a soap dish. Tajh made her way up the squeaky steps.

"Tajh, is that you?"

"Yes, Auntie!"

"How was the convention?" her aunt yelled from her room.

"It was good, I'm changing my clothes and leaving again. Do you need anything?"

"No, I'm fine."

She opened her door to see her room in the same mess she left it in. Clothes were scattered all over her bed from her being indecisive the night before. She didn't want to keep Khori waiting, so she grabbed a pair of jeans with rips in the front and a red T-shirt that said, 'The Marathon Continues,' in red, black, and green. Leaving her room, she snatched some gold hoops off her night stand and ran down the steps. Throwing on her fake Gucci flip flops with the matching sunglasses, she left out the door.

Khori plugged his address in the GPS and made a turn. Tajh sniffled a little, still noticing the smell of weed. Her bold personality forced her to ask about it. "So, do you sell or smoke it?"

Being caught off guard, Khori giggled, "What?"

He pulled up to a red light and the two eyeballed each other, Tajh had this semi smile on her face. "I didn't stutter. I said; "Do you smoke or do you sell?"

His clean white teeth were highlighted through his smile as he grasped on the gas pedal. "Why do you ask?"

"I can smell it."

"Really?"

"Yes, really."

He drove a couple more miles down the highway before finding the next exit to take. Pulling over at a gas station, he got out of the car and popped the trunk. "Tajh, come here."

This time, she opened her own door, got out, and walked to the back of the car. "I can trust you, right?"

"Maybe. You ain't got no dead bodies in there, do you?" He lifted open the trunk and pulled up the barrier where his spare tire was supposed to be. "OMG!" He shushed her and told her to lower her voice. The whole trunk was packed with small storage bags of weed, pounds and pounds of it. "Where did you get all of this?"

"My people. I go back and forth to get it and I wholesale it here."

"You wholesale that shit?"

"Yup. Told you, you can flip anything."

Putting the barrier back down, he shut his trunk and they got back in the car. Tajh had fucked drug dealers before but never really knew the game up close and personal. Them dudes kept her close but not close enough to put her on game. The whole time she lived in San Antonio, she was confined to certain areas. Not having a car and having to depend on Uber and Lyft didn't allow her to get around much. She enjoyed the mini road trip and all his childhood stories.

"We are here."

"Where are we?"

"Olmos Park."

"Wow, this is beautiful! You live here?"

"Yes."

She was thrilled and excited. She'd never seen a Black person living like this. She was used to hood rich guys with flashy cars, expensive jewelry, decked out mediocre homes, but nothing like this.

They drove up a stone driveway and in front of her was a house that sat on top of a hill overlooking the city. He pulled in front and proceeded to her door. "Thank you," she said with a small grin on her face. She immediately walked over to a fence and gazed down the hillside, watching the lights from the cars on the expressway.

"Are you thirsty?" he asked with his hands in his pockets.

She turned around. "What do you have to drink?"

"I think I have some Champagne and wine."

"You think? You don't know what you have?"

"Well, I'm not always here, I'm back and forth between here and Jamaica, so…"

"I'll take some Champagne."

"Coming right up." Khori went into the house and came back out with two glasses filled with Champagne. Tajh was still looking off into the sunset, watching the lights of the buildings across the highway. She had always dreamed of living like this—having a nice car and a beautiful home up on a hill. It was like someone else was living her dream. "Here you go madam." She took a glass of Champagne and continued to day dream.

Interrupted by a phone call, Khori excused himself and went back into the house. She stayed outside, thinking about her past and all the men she dealt with who weren't shit. This was the life she wanted. This was the life she needed. Right there, she made up her mind that she was gonna get put on and wasn't going to look back.

Tajh finished the last sip, and walked into the house. "I want you to coach me!" she demanded.

Finishing up his call, Khori smiled and put up his finger, telling her to give him a minute. She walked around his living room looking at the crystal decorations that surrounded the fireplace. None of the picture frames hanging up had actual pictures in it. "Sorry about that, that was business. Now, what were you saying?"

Picking up one of the pictures, she repeated herself, "I said, I want you to coach me. "

He sat back on the plush white sofa, crossing his legs. "Is that so?"

"Yes, I'm a fast learner; we can do business together. Look, I have had a shitty life and I deserve more." Khori didn't say anything, he just sat there looking at her. "Where are all your pictures?" Tajh asked, holding up one of the frames.

"They are put away." Her titter laugh made him question her. "Why did you laugh?"

"Who just has empty frames?"

He chuckled back. "Apparently, I do."

Tajh rolled her eyes and put the empty frames back as if she thought that was weird. "So, are you going to coach me or not?" She had seen this as her opportunity to make lots of money. For once in her life, her good looks weren't going to cut it. This type of lifestyle took brains and commitment and she didn't have anything to lose. Her boldness was either going to persuade him to teach her or scare him off. But she already knew he was interested in her, or why else would he have brought her to his house?

"Yes, I will teach you. But you must be willing to listen and be open minded." Tajh agreed and pulled out her hand to shake his. "First things first: You are a woman; use your sexuality to the best of your ability. No hand shaking. You will nod your head yes or give a seductive wink." Khori explained that women always have the upper hand. He implied the way a woman dresses and her gestures say a lot about a confident woman who knows her business. Of course, she knew all those things but if she was going to be making the kind of money he was making, she was going to do exactly what he told her to do.

Chapter II

"We are what we repeatedly do."

Her phone vibrated several times on the floor before she rolled over tirelessly trying to pick it up, almost falling off the bed. "Hello," she answered, not eager to know who was calling her at six a.m.

"Rise and shine, beautiful. Your internship starts now. Get dressed, I'll be there in twenty." With the sound of the dial tone in her ear, Khori hung up fast. She laid there for a few seconds slung over her bed thinking what he could possibly teach her this early in the morning. How could he be up this early? They stayed up most of the night over his house drinking Champagne and talking about old relationships. She was hung over and he should have been too.

She stumbled off the bed, walking into her small bathroom. Tajh had been in these predicaments before. Guys promised they were going to teach her how to get fast money, but they never did. They kept her around and gave her money, but there was always a price for it. This time, she knew she had to tread carefully, making sure she didn't mix business with pleasure. She was in a new state, starting over and this had to work. She had wasted so much time in the past and didn't want to repeat her mistakes.

She didn't know what to put on. Fumbling through her closet was starting to frustrate her. Should she put on a suit or just wear some regular shorts and a crop top? She chose the obvious. You could never go wrong with some tan slacks, a white t-shirt, and a black mid sleeve blazer. Not too relaxed and not too business-like. The doorbell rang and she still wasn't done getting dressed. She grabbed a black hair band and quickly wrapped it around her dreads. Her glossy pink lip gloss and gold hoops completed her look. She snatched a small red clutch purse off her vanity and headed down the steps.

Khori had gotten tired of waiting at the door, so he got back into his car. He sat there patiently, with his head down, waiting for her to come out. The sun was out. It was at least eighty degrees outside. He had on a pair of black and gold Versace sunglasses. His dark skin glistened in the driver seat with his long dreads dangling down his back. Green, black, and yellow beads draped his neck, representing his country. The necklace complemented his black muscle shirt.

Locking her door, Tajh began to apologize for her being late. "It's ok, get in."

"So, where are we going?" she asked as he opened the door for her.

"I have a surprise for you."

"What type of surprise? Is it about the business?"

"Yes, you have to have a certain look in order to gain trust from the clients, so we are going shopping."

Tajh let out a big smile. What woman doesn't like to go shopping? She wanted to make sure this was really about business, so she asked him the obvious. "Do you take all your interns shopping?"

He chuckled and said, "You are an investment for me. When you win, I win. Consider this as an advancement for now."

They went to several different stores, and each time, Khori paid cash, making sure he kept all the receipts. He schooled her on appearance and approach when it came to the difference in networking with men and women. It almost seemed like he was selling attitude instead of houses. He made it very clear that she wasn't pimping herself out but men will mostly buy from her if they are attracted to her and she is confident in the skill. Numbers were everything. Women and numbers were always an easy fit. When it came down to networking with other women, she had to be humble. Trying to find a common interest to seal the deal, even talking about family, kids, husbands future goals, anything to wheel them in, even if flirting was involved. Khori didn't do deals in low income neighborhoods, only in high end ones. That's how he made most of his money.

Over the next couple of months, Tajh had made enough money to purchase her own home. Back in her hometown, this type of money would have taken her years to get. Even the biggest drug dealers didn't have this type of money this soon. She didn't want to be too flashy. Still having street smarts, she didn't want to be marked. Living in a new town with new money made her an easy target, especially because she is a Black woman. She bought a small ranch style house a couple miles from her aunt's house. It wasn't a mansion, but it was hers. She decked out the two-bedroom house with furniture from a gallery in the West Bronx called Samira Furniture. She had always dreamed of having her own place with wall to wall leather and crystal accents. Her second bedroom was made into a walk in closet filled with all types of expensive shoes, clothes, and jewelry. This was the life she was meant to have. A milestone for her. The only problem was that she had nobody to tell about her accomplishments. No real family and no real friends. She plopped on her couch, wearing a long white Coco Chanel robe with matching slippers and a glass of Champagne in her hand, staring at her furniture, smiling eagerly, moving her head back and forth in disbelief that she had finally done it.

Khori convinced her it was time for her to get a car. He stressed that he wouldn't always be around to take her to appointments. She needed to drive something that showed power and wealth. With all the money she was making, a car would be a great addiction. Khori had already had a car picked out for her. She had never had someone look out for her as much as he did. It seemed all too fake. But who was she to complain about anything. With her past and the things, she went through, he was her night and shining armor.

Tajh drove away in a 2019 silver Bentley. Her hard work and dedication paid off. On her way back home, she received a phone call. "Hello," she answered through her car's Bluetooth.

"Hello beautiful." Kohri's voice made her produce a big smile. "How do you like your new ride?"

"I love it, and thank you so much, Kohri, for helping me."

"I didn't do anything. This was all you. But listen, I want to make a proposition, can you come to my house in an hour?"

"Yes, I can boss!"

"Ok, great, and wear something sexy."

Tajh floored it to her house. She wasn't sure if this was another business meeting and other men were going to be there or what. Normally, if he said that, she was meeting a man to do business with.

"Perfect," she said out loud, picking through the numerous dresses in her closet. She ran over to her oversized long length mirror and held up a red bodycon dress up against her breast. Admiring her beauty, she turned side to side contemplating if she wanted to wear it. She didn't have much time to get ready knowing how anal Kohri was about being late. The dress hugged every inch of her body, revealing her upper and lower back, stopping at her mid-calves. Her extensive selection of shoes left her standing there. She couldn't decide if she wanted to wear her black, ankle strapped, peep toe Vivier Marlene stiletto with crystals around the heels or her Gianvito Rossi hologram pointed ankle pumps. She tried both pairs on and decided to go with the black stilettos. Besides, they were new and she needed a reason to wear them. She quickly put on her jewelry, dabbed on her coach perfume, grabbed her car keys, and left.

She arrived at his house at exactly nine o'clock sharp. The light from the moon exposed her soft light skin. Her jewelry had a radiant sparkle which echoed a glare in her green eyes. She made sure to have that confident walk; she never knew who could be watching her. She didn't know Kohri was lurking, watching her get out the car through his blinds. He stood there with his Champagne, watching her firm ass bounce up and down in coordination with the movement of her breast.

Before she could ring the doorbell, he opened the door. He smiled and gestured to her to come in with his glass. "Wow, what's all this for; you having a party?" She was astounded, walking in seeing his living room surrounded with candles lit everywhere.

"No, we are celebrating."

"Celebrating what?" she responded in a mellow seductive tone, while walking slowly over to a table by a window that overlooked the view of the city. With her back facing him, she picked up a glass of Champagne and took a sip.

Kohri followed behind her, gently gliding his fingers down her back and responded, "Us."

"What about us?" she whispered, still gazing out the window.

He moved a little bit closer. She could smell his breath on her neck and could feel his dick enlarging up against her ass. "I want you to be my business partner." His seductive tone and hard dick led her to believe he wanted something else.

"Is that all you want?" She turned around and got on top of the table, opening up her legs. She had this provocative smile on her face. Kohri took it as an invitation.

He backed away, staring at her, loosening up his tie. One by one, he began removing his clothes. Tajh had never seen him with his shirt off before, but she knew he had muscles from them bulging out through his cotton shirts. He stood there with his dreads hanging down his back, his masculine chest, his rock hard dick sticking straight out, and his dress socks on. She was astounded. She continued to gander at him, drinking her Champagne, not moving an inch from the table. She knew how the game worked. She pretended to not be too pressed, although she wanted it just as bad as him. She turned sideways, lifting her right leg on top of the table, letting her left leg dangle off the table. She untied the strap from around her neck and let the top part of her dress slump down to her small waist.

Kohri's smile disappeared and his adrenaline took over. He rushed over to Tajh with his hard cock swinging back and forth. Getting on his knees, he began kissing Tajh's left thigh. Gripping her inner leg with her mouth and eyes close, she let out a large moan, "Ahhh!" Her head drifted back. The further he went up her thigh, the more she began to whimper. "Mmmh... Ohh!" Her legs were wide open and her shaved pussy was staring him in the face. Gently kissing the top of her pussy, he began working his way down. She let out brief shrieks. His lips connected with her pussy lips. Burying his face deeper, he lapped on her clitoris with his tongue. His moist tongue dampened her pussy. He could tell she enjoyed it because she grabbed his head with both her hands and held his head still. He stayed there squatting, his dick straight out, thrusting it back and forth with his hands, licking her pussy, and sucking the juice that came sprouting out.

Tajh knew it was wrong to mix business with pleasure but she couldn't help herself. This man took care of her, put her on, helped her get her life together, and he was so damn fine. Khori stood up and picked up Tajh, put her over his right shoulder and began walking to the bedroom. Her titties dangled across his back and her ass hung out right by his face. He smacked it a couple of times and wiggled it back and forth, enjoying the flow of the way her ass vibrated.

He pushed open the door to his bedroom and threw her on the king sized bed. Slipping off his socks, he climbed on top of her, sucking and licking her breast. With his other hand, he slid his fingers into her pussy, making sure she was still wet for him. Turning her over, making her get on all fours, he pulled her ass back closer to him to make sure her feet were planted on the floor. It was clear he wanted to devour her pussy. He grabbed a handful of her dreads, bending her over and pushing her head down into the bed. With her ass up against his legs, he grabbed his nine-inch brick hard black dick and eased it into her wet pussy. Pushing and pulling her ass up against him, the sound of her ass smacking up against him turned him on even more. He took short slow strokes, watching her come spread like jelly all over him. With every hard stroke that he plunged into her, she'd let out a sound, "Ohhh… Ahhh… Aahhh." He knew she enjoyed it as much as he did. She tilted her head, watching every single facial expression when he thrust his dick in and out of her.

Khori loved having power, being in control fed his ego. He pulled his dick out of her pussy and guided her to turn around. He pushed her down, making her knees bend into a squat-like position. She came face to face with his dick and her come all over it. She could smell her own aroma. He was still holding her dreads in his hand. She looked up at him, wanting him to direct her on what to do next. He took a step closer, "Open," he demanded in a forceful but subtle tone. She obliged. Tajh opened her mouth and he took another step forward, stuffing her mouth with his dick. She began to gag as he was trying to fit the whole thing in her mouth. Spit began to slobber out her mouth as she gasped for air. He watched her as she struggled. With a slow movement, her lips clasped around his dick, establishing a rhythm. "That's it," he whispered. He pushed and pulled her head, clinging on to her locs, watching his dick go in and out her mouth. "Yeah baby… Yeah baby…" he sang a couple times. Enjoying her jaw breaking head, he tilted his head back with his dreads touching his firm muscular ass and began mumbling to himself. "Ahhhhh… Yeahhh, that's it… Right there… Suck it… Take all of it… Ahhh…"

Tajh enjoyed it too. The sounds Khori murmured, reassured her he was enjoying every bit of it. She loved a man who could take control. This brought the freak out in her. She played with her pussy while looking up, watching him enjoy face fucking her. The more he moaned, the more she moaned. He picked up the pace, guiding her head back and forth a little faster, and pushing his dick deeper in her throat. His moaning got louder. "Ahhh! Yeah! Fuck! Suck it! Ahhh… Suck it!" She could feel the veins in his dick throbbing. She knew that meant he was about to come. One thing Tajh didn't do was swallow. She thought that shit was nasty. She didn't want it in her mouth or nowhere near her face. Each time she tried to move her head back away from his hard dick, he would grip her head even tighter. "Ahhhh, AHHHH AHHHHHH!!!!" He got louder and louder, pumping his hips harder and faster. Tajh began to gag again but this time, he wasn't letting loose. Staring down at her, still controlling her head, he grabbed his dick, pulled it out her mouth and started squirting his nut all over her face.

She sat on her knees gazing at him with come dripping down her face. *I can't believe this mothafucka,* she said in her head. She remained poised and didn't want to seem angry. After all, he was her plug for getting money. She stood up and walked to the bathroom to clean herself up. Glancing at herself in the mirror, she questioned her own motive, knowing she didn't want to fall for this man but also recognizing it was too late.

"You okay in there?" Khori shouted through the door.

"Yeah, I'm good." She finished wiping his come off her face and left the bathroom. Khori greeted her at the end of the hall wearing nothing but a white towel that wrapped around his waist. He slowly put his arms around her and gently kissed her on her forehead. Tajh stood there for a moment taking in the aroma of his manly cologne. She closed her eyes thinking about all the men she had dated in the past. They all had money and bought her anything she wanted but never gave her what she needed. In that moment, Khori had given her something she had craved for, for so long, intimacy.

"So, where do we go from here?" Tajh asked in a sweet, subtle voice.

"Now, we make money together." Khori smiled and took Tajh by the hand. "Come here, I want to show you something." He led her into another room that was empty.

She giggled, "Umh, I don't see anything."

He turned around and grabbed her face with one hand, staring into her eyes with a seductive look. "I want you to move in with me."

Tajh tried to interrupt him, "But–"

"But nothing. I'm not asking, I'm telling you. If we are going to be business partners, I need you to be right by my side at all times. I need you to learn the business, plus I like you a little."

She blushed a little, trying not to smile. "Okay, I think I can do that." Khori grabbed both her hands and kissed them. "So you only like me a little bit?" she asked jokingly.

"Well, maybe a lot." They both started laughing.

A month had passed and Tajh was living her best life. Never in a million years did she think she would own her own home, drive a Bentley and have three credit cards all worth over thirty thousand each, rocking expensive clothing and jewelry. Most of the things she brought to Texas were bought by a nigga or stolen from the outlets from her friends who were boosters. Back home, the homies put on fronts. Driving around in their baby momma's car or a rental, trying to showboat and act like the shit was theirs. But everybody knew that shit wasn't theirs. There's no come up on selling nickel bags of weed and bootlegged movies. You had to be pushing weight to make the kind of money Tajh was making. And even if they did make that kind of money, niggas didn't flash that shit. Your own man would hustle with you and turn around and rob your ass within the same hour. The real hustle was to make your bread and keep quiet. There were levels to the hustle. Never shit where you lay. Niggas would hustle right out of their momma's house or baby momma's. The next thing you know, they are waking up to a shotty pointed at their head. The game couldn't be trusted and neither could these niggas. Shit was so fucked up you couldn't even trust your own baby momma. These hoes would set them up in a heartbeat. Just to turn around and be compensated for a twenty sack, a pack of squa's, and maybe some weak ass dick. But not Tajh, she was hood but knew how to manipulate these dudes for their information. She was very careful that she didn't get caught up in any drama. She never really fucked with the females but when she needed to, she knew how to finesse them too. The one thing she had learned by being in the streets was that the product doesn't sell itself. In most cases, Tajh was the product, and she was gonna get what she was worth.

Khori called Tajh to tell her he had some important people coming over, a silent business partner, and wanted her to wear something sexy for the occasion. Normally, Tajh would have a problem with Khori telling her how to dress, but once again, she trusted his judgment. "What time does the meeting start?" she asked.

"Be here by eight p.m. I have some heavy hitters here and we could possibly be doing some business in Jamaica."

She was excited to finally get a chance to meet some of his business partners. She knew this meeting was important and wanted to look her best. Khori was good at springing surprises on her at short notice, but she made sure she was on point with whatever he needed her to do. Even though being submissive wasn't in her nature, she made exceptions for him.

She arrived at their house at exactly eight p.m. sharp just as he instructed. The front of the house was filled with expensive looking cars in their driveway. Greeting her and opening her door was a valet.

She stepped out in a pair of nine hundred dollar pointed black patent leather stiletto heels that was embellished with crystals that cuffed her ankles. With a mid-leg, spaghetti strapped, satin black dress that hugged her thighs, she exited the car and gave the keys to the valet. Her hair was twisted up in a bun and her crystal earrings dangled down to her shoulders. Her breast, firm and perky, showed just enough cleavage to get the attention she wanted. His.

Grabbing a glass of Champagne from the servers that were outside, she smiled, gulped it down in one swallow, took a deep breath and sashayed her pretty little ass in. Not trying to look eager or thirsty, she glanced around the crowded noisy living room looking for Khori. She spotted him in the corner talking with a couple of guys. He glanced over at her and waved for her to come over. She slowly walked towards him. With the sounds of everyone talking, it was hard to hear what Khori and the other men were talking about. "Fellas, I would like to introduce you to Tajh," he said, grabbing her hand. "This is my mentee. I am teaching her the ins and outs of real estate," he said, smiling at her.

"Hello," she responded, looking at each and every one of them.

"Hello Tajh. My name is Carl and I am Khori's business partner," one of them said, taking her hand and kissing the back of it. "You look stunning my dear."

"Thank you," she replied, thinking to herself, *I thought I was his business partner.*

Another White gentleman also responded, "Tajh, I'm Dave. It's a pleasure to meet you. You have a great mentor on your hands. I should know, I taught him everything he knows." They both giggled.

"It's nice to meet you, Dave."

"Well, we have some mingling to do, so we will meet up later," Carl said.

Khori turned around, staring at Tajh, "You look fabulous. When I said get something sexy, I didn't expect all this."

"Is it too much?"

"No, it's just right. You have all the guys in here wanting my lady. I might get jealous."

"Oh, I'm your lady now?" she replied, blushing.

"Only if you want to be." Khori flagged one of the hostesses to bring over drinks.

"So, what exactly is this party for?"

"Well, my dear, we are expanding. These are some heavy hitters and I plan for us to purchase property in countries like Dubai, Mexico, and the Dominican Republic. I also plan to go back home and I want you to come with me. I'm ready to buy and sell commercial properties in some low income communities and turn them into Airbnb condos. These men here have the capital that I need to do so."

"But what about the people who already live there, where would they go?" she asked out of concern.

"This will be a great opportunity for the natives because it will bring money to their community, plus they will have first choice for job openings at the condos."

Tajh recognized the game a mile away. But this was a bigger field she was playing in. The only difference between the hustlers at home and the hustlers here was money and manipulation. She knew it was about who you know and how you talked to them. Khori did just that. He could talk his way in and out of a deal just like he talked his way into her panties. But she admired that about him. He knew his craft and knew how to fit in with these White mothafuckas. He spoke their language—money! The more she watched him work them, the more she fell for his masculinity. The power of having power in any situation. He walked with confidence. The way his eyes presented what he was thinking. Never moving too fast and always thinking before he spoke. This slick bastard had her wide open and wanting more. If she could be in his skin, she would. She sat there with her legs crossed, admiring him, drinking, thinking about a possible future with him. Although she had heard all the game from men, no one could outdo Khori. Not intimidated, she saw how all the women at the party looked and touched him. She didn't care. She knew there was a possibility he'd hit them off once or twice. Tajh wanted what she wanted and Tajh always got what she wanted. She thought to herself, *These bitches ain't got nothing on me.* She wasn't the jealous type, but she knew to keep her mouth shut and her eyes and ears open, because a man is still a man.

After four drinks of Grand Marnier, Tajh was hit. Barely able to stand, Khori came over, put her arm around his neck, and helped her to the room. "Where did everyone go?" she asked, slurring her words.

"They left, it's just us, beautiful."

"Oh, well I had a great time. Everyone was so friendly. I love your friends."

He laughed, "And they love you too, baby. Listen, I have some business papers for you to sign, do you think you're up to it?" he asked, helping her on the bed.

"What kind of business papers. You're so cute," she said, touching his face.

He laughed, "Thank you, babe. Nothing much. Now that we are partners, it's just some liability papers." Khori walked to his night stand and pulled out a pen. With no hesitation, he put the pen in her hand and helped her sign three pieces of paper on the dotted lines. Tajh laid there with her back across the bed, passed out.

"Did she sign?"

"Shhhh, you're gonna wake her up."

Khori tipped toed out the door. Carl gave Khori a glass of Champagne, "Let's make a toast. To us and all the fucking money we are about to make." The two held up their glasses and began drinking. "Well, that went well. I'm gonna go, I have an early flight in the morning." Carl put his glass on the table and proceeded to walk out.

"I'll walk you out."

Tajh's phone began to vibrate on the bed, waking her out of her deep sleep. Noticing Khori was gone, she got up, calling for him. "Khori, babe, where you at?" Staggering, trying to keep her balance, she knocked over his lamp in the room. Barely being able to see, she made her way out to the front of the house. "Khori, babe what are you doing? Are you peeing outside?" Khori was standing three feet from his fence that overlooked the beautiful city. He shifted his back to see Tajh walking towards him.

"Oh, hey baby. Just stay right there. I'll be back in a minute."

"Why are you taking a piss outside? Come in and give me some dick. I wanna taste it." She laughed with spit coming out her mouth.

"Go back in. I said I will be there in a minute," he demanded. Tajh turned around and waved her hand at him and stumbled back into the house.

"Did she see us?" Carl mumbled while squatting down with Khori's dick in his mouth.

"No, I don't think so. Keep going, I'm about to bust. Ummmh... Ummmh..." Khori moaned, while holding Carl's head, pumping back and forth. "Ahhhh... Ahhhh... Ahhhh.... That's it... You love this dick... Take all of it..." he whispered out loud. Carl unzipped his pants and pulled out his cock and began jerking it back and forth. Losing his balance, he fell to his knees and began pumping while jerking off to the sounds of Khori's moans.

"Get up now!" Khori demanded, pulling Carl up off the ground and pushing him into the fence. "Turn around." Khori pulled down Carl's pants, spat in his hand and began rubbing his dick to get it lubed up. Khori bent down, opened up Carl's but cheeks and began licking his ass hole. He stuck his fingers in his hole to open it up more and then stuck his hard dick right in Carl's ass. Carl clutched the fence and bent over a little more to make sure Khori's dick was all the way in. Khori thrusted back and forth fast and hard. Carl enjoyed Khori's dick so much the noises of his enjoyment got louder and louder, making Tajh come back outside to see where all the noises were coming from.

Tajh came tumbling out the house, trying to catch her balance. "Khori, come in, what's all the–" She stood there, watching Khori bang Carl's ass up against the fence. Not knowing Tajh was standing there, Khori continued to pump harder and harder until he busted all over Carl's ass. In shock, Tajh stood there with her hands over her mouth and around her stomach trying not to make a sound. Tears began rolling down her eyes. Khori fixed his clothes and turned around to see Tajh standing there. "What the fuck, what is this, are you gay!" she screamed.

"Baby, wait. Let me explain." He tried to walk over to Tajh. She began throwing up the food and liquor from the party.

"No! Get the fuck away from me, you faggot! You fucking faggot!"

Khori turned towards Carl, "Just call me when you land, I'll handle this."

Carl fixed his clothes and proceeded to his car. Tajh ran back into the house in rage, screaming. "Fuck, fuucckk! I knew this was too good to be true. How did I not see this?" She ran into the room, snatching her clothes out the closet, throwing them on the bed.

"Baby, baby, listen to me…" He grabbed her, trying to calm her down.

"Why? Why, Khori, huh? Why would you do this to me? You're gay. I thought that was your business partner, you fucking liar!" She began punching him in the chest. Khori grabbed her and hugged her tight.

"I know, babe. I'm sorry but there is just some things you have to do in this business."

She pulled away, "No, no, you don't get to hurt me and heal me. There's nothing you can say to fix this!" She grabbed her suit case and threw her clothes in it.

"I'm not gay!" he said angrily.

"Oh, yeah, well tell that shit to Carl. Tell that shit to my heart. I know what I saw. You sure as hell looked gay to me back there!"

Khori got up and poured himself a drink. "Baby, please listen to me!" he pleaded.

"You've got one fucking minute!" She continued to pack.

"I'm not gay. He is a business partner, but he is gay. He wouldn't do the deal if I didn't please him. Baby, this deal is worth over a million dollars. I couldn't let that offer go. I had to do what I needed to do, for us. This game is ruthless and sometimes we have to do things to get ahead. There are gonna be times that I'm gonna need you to do some things that you don't want to. Listen, I understand if you want to go, but I've been in this game for a long time. I grew up dirt poor. No shoes, no clothes, no food to eat for weeks. I refuse to go back to that because of the stereotypes that people place on us."

She stopped packing and turned around. "Did you fucking forget how I grew up? I didn't have anyone. I went from home to home. At least you had family. You didn't see me out here tricking and eating coochie!" she screamed.

"We are no different, Tajh. Yes, I know what you've been through, but we are no different. You fucked these hood niggas and got what out of it, huh? What did you get? Some jewelry, a couple of hundred bucks, some weed, heart break, disease?"

"Khori, we are not the same, and don't you dare judge me!"

"You're absolutely right. We are not the same. Cause if I do something I don't want to do, at least I get a bag, right! That's the terminology you all use. See, that's the difference between people like me and people like you. I don't fuck for free; I fuck to be freed. So, if you're gonna leave, don't ever come back."

Khori took his drink and left the room. Tajh couldn't believe he was out here tricking for money. Her heart was broken. It was one thing to trick with a female, but another dude. No, that didn't sit right with her, as fine as he was. She used to hear all the time about guys tricking down in Atlanta, the ones on the downlow. But this was a whole other world that she wasn't used to. She couldn't help but to be a realist and understand Khori had some truth to what he was saying. It definitely costs to be on top. And Tajh was definitely a top bitch. It fucked her up that she fell for him. He gassed her up like the niggas she used to fuck with back home. Only difference between them and Khori, he actually broke bread with her ass. She felt him on some real shit, not wanting to be poor again. Mothafuckas will break bread with a total stranger and watch their own struggle. Maybe this was how they did it in the big league. Give a little ass and take a lot of dough. At least Khori wasn't naive to the hustle. He understood what needed to be done in order to get what he wanted. Definitely a tough pill to swallow. But damn, she fell for this nigga. How the fuck didn't she see this shit coming? Blinded by the charm, the money, the lifestyle and definitely the dick, that's how. *But why me?* she thought, questioning if she'd gotten soft since she'd been in Texas, turning into a simp.

She took a deep breath and raised up off the bed, contemplating on what she was going to say to Khori. She would have told any other man to kick rocks, but there was something about validity and accountability that slapped her right in the face. He accepted who he was, a straight hustla who was comfortable with being uncomfortable when it came to getting what he wanted.

"Hey, can we talk?" she said, leaning on the living room wall.

"Sure," he said, taking a sip of Ciroc. "Have a seat."

She walked over to him and sat next to him on the couch. "Listen, I understand everything you just said. I apologize for judging you. I guess what really bothered me was that you did that with another guy. I felt stupid. Is Carl someone I have to worry about? I mean, do you do these things often?" she asked in a concerning voice.

"No and yes. This was the first time I have done this with Carl, but I have done it a few other times."

She lowered her head in disbelief. "So what about us, where do we go from here?"

"Where do you want to go? I was very honest with you. This is only business for me, nothing more. I guess what I'm saying is…" he leaned forward towards her and caressed her cheek, looking into her eyes. "Baby, I'm in love with you."

Tajh lowered her head and began blushing. "I'm in love with you too."

Continuing to caress her cheek, he scooted closer to her and gently placed his lips onto hers. Giving her the reassurance that she needed, he landed a subtle kiss. Khori knew it was too soon to arouse her, he felt like he needed to earn her trust back. So, he did what any other omitter would do, he laid down on the couch and cuddled with Tajh, holding her tightly in his arms until the next morning.

Chapter III

"Illusion is the first of all pleasures."

The buzzing of Khori's phone vibrated on the table, waking him up. He picked it up, squinting his eyes looking to see who was calling. "Hello," he asked, yawning. "Oh, hey, how are you?" "Today, really? Ok, I'll be on the next flight."

"Who was that?" Tajh asked, yawning and stretching, getting up off the couch.

"That was my other hook up from Jamaica. There's some property out there I have been trying to get my hands on and they are ready to sell. I need to be on the next flight so they don't sell to anyone else," he said, standing up.

"I've never been to Jamaica," Tajh said in a low tone, hoping Khori would ask her to join him. "Really, you've never been?"

"No!"

"Where have you been?"

"I've traveled but not out of the country."

"Umh, so you don't have a passport?"

"No," she replied, shaking her head.

He stood there for a minute with his hand on his cheek, trying to figure out a solution. He snapped his finger. "Okay, I've got it. Go pack your bag and get dressed, I know someone."

"What do you mean you know someone. Babe, I don't have a passport."

"I'm gonna get you one. Just go pack," Khori picked up his unfinished drink that was left on the table from the night before and swallowed the rest. He rolled up his sleeves and left the room. Tajh didn't ask any more questions. She got up and went to pack her clothes.

Tajh came out of the room forty-five minutes later. "I'm ready." She had two Louis Vuitton suitcases stuffed with clothes.

"Damn girl, what you got in there, the whole closet?"

She stood there looking sexy in her matching Louis Vuitton jumpsuit that hugged all her curves. Her breasts were perky sitting up firmly, showing cleavage. Her solid ass sitting up high and her legs looking smooth and toned.

"Shut up. A woman must have options," she said jokingly. "Besides, you didn't say how long we were going to be there anyway."

Khori grabbed her bags and went to the car. He popped the trunk and put both her bags next to his. He opened Tajh's door so she could get in. "Hold on, baby, let me set the alarm before we leave." He closed her door and ran back into the house to set the alarm. "All set, let's go."

The two left to go get a passport made for Tajh. She was excited to finally be traveling out of the country. Having a fake passport didn't scare her as much as actually riding on a plane. Khori gave her the do's and don'ts of Jamaica. "Ok, when we land, let me do all the talking."

"Why?" she asked. "I can handle myself."

"I know you can, but they can spot tourists a mile away. They will try to sell you everything under the sun, and there are a lot of scam artists lurking around the terminal. Do you trust me?" he asked, looking at her.

"Yes, I trust you."

The two checked in their bags and went through airport security. "I think our plane is this way," he pointed. They got to their terminal just in time as people were already boarding the plane.

"I'm so nervous."

"What are you nervous about?"

"I've never been on a plane before, what if something goes wrong?"

"Like what?"

"I don't know. Like what if we get high jacked or the plane crashes?"

"Girl, you watch too many movies. There's nothing to worry about, plus I'm here to protect you."

"You can't protect me from no falling airplane."

"Girl, get on this plane." He shoved her to get on.

After seven hours and thirty-two minutes, and one layover of two hours and forty-two minutes, they finally arrived in Kingston, Jamaica. "How do I say hi in your language?" she asked excitingly.

"Umh… Hi," he replied. "Babe, we speak English. Just broken English with an accent," he laughed.

"I knew that, I was just testing you." She turned around and walked away. Khori went to baggage claim and got their luggage while Tajh stood out front taking selfies of herself. "We all set?" she asked, "Let's take a selfie." She tried to take a picture with Khori but he declined. "Maybe later babe. Let's get a taxi and be on the road.

Where we are going is about forty minutes from here." He flagged down a taxi and the two headed out.

Tajh sat there quietly looking out the window, admiring the view, taking pictures of the big houses and acres of land. "So what area is this?"

"This is Cheery Gardens."

"It's beautiful here," she said, gazing out the window. Their taxi slowed down, turning into a resort. "Are we here?" she asked with excitement.

He touched her leg, "Yes."

They pulled up to the resort. There were three men standing in front with their hands crossed, waiting for the taxi to park. They opened both doors and grabbed the luggage from the trunk. Tajh and Kohri were greeted by a beautiful brown skinned woman. Her natural skin looked silky, as if she didn't wear makeup. The song, *I woke up like this,* came to mind when Tajh looked at her. Her long black hair flowed with the wind as she walked closer. *Is her body real?* Tajh questioned. He was fixated on her coca cola bottled shaped body. The peach colored two piece bodycon dress exposed her flat stomach, broad hips, perky breast and firm legs. Not any cellulite on site. *Who the fuck is this bitch?* Tajh wondered as she hugged Khori.

"Brotha, I have missed you," she said in her Jamaican accent, giving him a hug.

Whew, her insecurity was about to get the best of her.

"Sistah, I missed you too," he responded, grabbing her hand while walking over to Tajh.

"I see the state's has taken away your accent. You sound like one of them now."

Kohri smiled, "Sistah, I would like you to meet my business partner, Tajh." Tajh extended her hand for a hand shake but Khor's sister just stood there smiling. "Tajh, this is my baby sister, Erzulie." I apologize for her rudeness. She is not used to me bringing women home."

Tajh felt uncomfortable, like an outsider. But felt the need to break the awkward silence. "That's a beautiful name, what does it mean?"

Erzulie broke her silence and walked closer to Tajh, standing directly in front of her. She broke her smile and gave this intimidating look. "It's Haitian and means…" she got closer to Tajh, whispering in her ear, "goddess." She turned around and started walking towards the hallway. Tajh stood there, wondering what the fuck just happened. This bitch was on some weird shit. But Tajh left the hood back in the States.

"Mr. Khori, your room is ready. You can follow me now." The two proceeded to follow the man. "I'm confused, is this a resort, or…"

Khori laughed. "Yes, it is. My family owns it, which means we can come and go as we please." She was so impressed. They both followed the bellhop to their rooms. It was like a movie scene, just how he opened both doors. This wasn't just a room; it was a whole house in one section. The floors were white marble with splashes of gold. The bed was an oversized king bed filled with plush pillows, silk sheets, and what felt like chinchilla fur as a bedspread. The windows were enormous with a balcony attached overlooking the ocean. Tajh continued to walk through the rooms, amazed by such beauty. She got to her favorite room, which was the bathroom. The bathroom was just as big as the bedroom. It featured two showers and a jacuzzi. The showers both had shower heads that draped down from the ceiling and water that came out of the wall. She stood thinking about the various ways her and Khori could make love. Not to mention a powder area and a built-in sauna. She knew right there that she'd connected with the right person.

Khori watched her from the bedroom exploring the bathroom, turning on the water from the shower. She turned around and watched Khori watching her. She took this as an opportunity to seduce him. She pulled out her phone and scrolled through her playlist. *Ain't nothing wrong with a little Janet to set the mood,* she thought. She found *Anytime, anyplace* and pressed play. As soon as the song began, she took a couple of slow exotic steps to the doorway separating the bathroom and bedroom. Keeping eye contact, Khori watched her slowly take off her Louis Vuitton top and slipped off her pants, standing there in just her black thong and bra that cuffed her breast. Slowly turning around and bending over, she picked up her clothes and placed them on the sink. Khori sat there with his rock hard dick staring at her. Tajh signaled him to come towards her with her head. He stood up off the bed and snatched his shirt off. His masculine build made Tajh excited. She took two of her fingers and started playing with her pussy, making it wet, watching him get undressed. Khori stood there in a stance, shoulders broad, dreads up in a ponytail, dick hard as a brick, ready to devour her pussy. "Anytime, anyplace," came the sound of Janet's voice echoing through the sound of the running water from the shower. Tajh turned around and opened the shower door, ready to walk through. Khori shook his head and said, "No, not in there." His deep toned voice indicated control, something Tajh loved. He grabbed her by the waist, turned her around, picking her up and placing her ass on the edge of the sink. The steam from the shower fogged up the window and mirrors. Looking into her eyes, he slowly pulled her panties off. "Is this what you want?" He stood there, holding his erected dick in his hands.

"Yes," she replied in a low tone.

He shook his head, "Naw." He squatted down until he was face to face with her pussy. With a tight grip, he placed both his hands on the outer side of the sink to hold his stance and began licking her pussy. With her legs spread wide open, she leaned back with her back and head smashed against the mirror. She held his head as she continued to moan each time he stuck his tongue into her slippery pussy. Each time her pussy juice ran down, he licked it off and sipped it right out, as if he was sipping a cup of hot coffee. Tajh's legs began to shake when he forced his tongue directly on her clitoris, moving it gently in a slow circular motion. Ahhhh..." She closed her eyes as if she couldn't take the pleasurement, slamming the back of her head up against the mirror, cracking it. "Ahh, ahhhh," she let out loud moans. He sucked and slurped every time his tongue felt her pussy wet up again. Khori stood up off the floor. With her legs still open, he slightly stuck the tip of his dick in, moving it around in small circles, taunting her. His throaty voice asked, "You ready?" Before Tajh could answer, he slid his meaty dick in her, filling up any space, leaving no room for her pussy to breathe. It was like her soul left her body and she took her last breath as she gasped for air when Khori inserted himself. Her eyes rolled up and her sclera was the only thing visible. Khori took both his hands, grabbed her ass and scooped her off the bathroom countertop. Tajh held on tightly around his neck while he bounced her jiggly ass up and down on his dick. Looking at the mirror, Khori watched as the ripples of her butt moved freely every time Tajh's body pumped up and down on him. He enjoyed watching the body movements of women and listening to the sounds of each movement. It made him feel superior. It was art to him. It boosted his ego to watch himself perform and see the reactions on their faces.

Getting ready to come, he clutched her ass tighter, closed his eyes and let out a loud sound, "Ahhhhhh... Ahhhhhh..." He pumped harder and harder. Small increments of sweat began rolling down his face as he breathed heavily, trying to catch his breath. His arm muscles swelled up from holding Tajh so long. "Ahhhhh... That's it." Tajh continued to hold on to Khori with her eyes closed, kissing on his neck while he unloaded himself in her.

He stood there for a moment breathing heavily. "Ok, we need to shower and get dressed. I'm meeting a client in the city and you can chill with my sister until I get back." He kissed her on the forehead and got in the shower. Tajh wasn't too happy that he wanted her to chill with his sister. She sensed from the looks she was giving her that she wasn't too fond of her. Tajh knew the shade when she saw it. But she decided to put her pride aside and obliged to his demands.

Tajh wanted to look classy. She wanted Khori's sister to know she was the real deal, that she could handle her own. She was serious about getting her money and that meant picking everyone's brain who Khori was connected to, being strategic about how she moved, how she talked, and even how she dressed. She had to leave that hood mentality behind and be open to how these rich motherfuckers got down. A world she wasn't ready for.

She wrapped her dreads up in a high bun. She pulled out a white sheer bikini with a black Coco Chanel wrap around with matching shades and heels to match. She lotioned up her body and applied her ruby red lipstick. "Perfection," she said, admiring herself in the bathroom mirror. She grabbed her white Louis Vuitton clutch purse and proceeded out the door.

"Floor 1," the elevator attendant said, reaching the first floor. Tajh adjusted her glasses and took a deep breath before stepping out of the elevator. "There she is... Gorgeous," Tajh said with such delight, approaching Khori's sister, attempting to hug her.

Erzulie stepped back and immediately started introducing Tajh to the other women. "Tajh, this is Gabrielle, Kaleisha, and Amancia. Gabrielle is the on-call manager of the hotel, Kaleisha is the guest attendant, and Amancia is in charge of Public Relations."

"Nice to meet you. Nice to meet you," Tajh said with a big smile on her face, shaking the women's hands.

"Shall we ladies?" Erzulie said, holding her hands out. They all began following her out the lobby doors. When they got outside, there was a black limousine waiting for them. A tall, dark and handsome guy with a gray suit stood there with a tray holding white wine with the door open, greeting them one at a time.

"Ladies," he said as he handed each of them a glass as they entered the limo. She shut the door after Tajh and proceeded to the driver's door.

"So, where are we going?" Tajh asked, sipping her wine.

"To make some money," Erzulie said with a slight grin.

"Oh, I like money," Tajh responded. "Good, cause where we're going isn't for the cheap, and I hope you brought plenty. Cause why, ladies?"

"Scared money don't make money," they all said out loudly together, toasting their drinks. Tajh continued to sip her wine and watched as the ladies conversated with each other with their accents.

Tajh remained quiet throughout the whole drive, watching and studying their every move; how they talked, how they drank, and even how they sat, hoping she could learn and one day be a part of this elite group of women. She came a long way from living in the hood to now sitting in a limousine with some rich Black Jamaican women.

"We are here, ladies!" Erzulie yelled with excitement as the limo pulled up to a building that appeared to be abandoned. It looked like an old theater, with boards in place of the windows. Remnants of trash were in front along with a couple of homeless people that sat on cardboard boxes. It smelled like urine as soon as they got out. "Is this where we're going?" Tajh asked, while being hesitant to get out.

"Yes, illusions is the first of all pleasures," Erzulie said, walking up to one of the homeless men. "Do you have five hundred dollars you can spare?" the homeless man asked, holding out his cup, being careful not to give eye contact.

"Yes." Erzulie took out a bunch of one hundred dollar bills, counted them in front of the homeless man out loud and placed them in his cup.

"You may enter," he said as he pressed a button on his watch. Both doors opened up and they followed Erzulie into the building. They walked down a narrow hallway with bright lights and big mirrors on the wall outlined with frames. Tajh stopped at one to look at herself to make sure her hair and makeup was still intact. As she got closer, she noticed it was a two-way mirror and could see that someone was behind it staring at her.

"This way please," Erzulie snapped her fingers, reassuring Tajh to follow her.

They came to an elevator. This time, there was a woman who appeared to be homeless. "How much is your wager?" The three ladies all took out three hundred each and gave it to the lady. Tajh followed and gave her three hundred as well. The homeless woman took out a camera, took everyone's picture and handed them a card with three numbers on it.

"What's this for?" Tajh asked.

"This is how you will collect your winnings if you win," Erzulie explained. Ding, the large golden elevator doors opened and they all turned around and walked on. Tajh was confused and worried at the same time, hoping this wasn't no cult shit she saw on television, but trusting her gut and the fact it was Khori's sister. She knew he wouldn't put her in any harm's way.

"Going down," the elevator said as it began to slowly move down from floor to floor. "Floor G." The doors opened and they all walked off. Once again, they walked down another hallway. But Tajh could hear other people as they walked past other entry way doors to other theaters. She could hear moaning. They came to a door that had the words Sex Capsule lit up over the door. As they entered the small dark theater, Tajh could see most of the seats were filled up. There was a stage with three beds that sat next to each other. "Take your seats," a gentleman said, as he walked around, handing out envelopes. The five found their seats at the very top.

"Thank you," Tajh said, taking her envelope. She opened it up immediately, eager to see what was inside. It was a small white piece of paper with six names on it. Three names were men and the other three were women's names. The attendant made his way to the stage to introduce these people who were just standing there. As he said their name, they walked out in front one by one with some type of gesture or hand wave as he introduced them. Two of the men who were on stage were White and the others were Black. Tajh couldn't help but to notice one of the men looked like the driver that drove them to the theater. Having on different clothes, it enhanced his body type. He stood there as his dark tone glistened from the lights that beamed off his body. His masculinity showed through the white T-shirt he had on and his leg depth showed he worked out often if not every day. Mesmerized by his beauty, she wasn't listening to what the attendant was explaining.

"Snap, snap," Erzulie snapped her fingers in Tajh's face. "Are you listening, dear. If you don't pay attention, you'll lose. Now, pick a name."

Tajh checked off Badrick. *Why not?* she thought to herself. She quickly wrote down the three numbers from the card she had gotten and slid the paper back into the envelope. The attendant walked around to each guest and collected them. She happily handed hers to him and sat back as the lights on the stage dimmed lower. "Are they some type of performers?"

"No," Gabrielle said, sitting back with a grin on her face. Soft instrumental music began to play through the speakers and as her eyes was fixated on Badrick, he started slowly taking off his clothes. They all did.

"What the fuck!"

"Shsssshh," a woman in front turned around angrily.

Tajh sat there with her mouth opened in shock while watching the six people on stage give each other oral. She peeked over at the other women, watching them slide their hands up their skirts and dresses, pleasuring themselves as they watch the people on stage pleasure each other. The sound of the music faded and she could hear them on stage moaning through the theater speakers. Badrick stood in front of the third bed. His cock appeared to be nine inches long. Tajh was fixated on it while one of the women was on her hands and knees deep throating his dick. Another woman walked over and was on her knees as well, waiting for her turn to deep throat him too. On the other bed were two guys and the other woman. They both were taking turns, ramming there dicks into both holes. One was behind her and the other was in front, controlling her head. He was pulling his dick in and out, smacking her from time to time. Tajh was shocked that anything like what she was seeing actually existed. This was the shit she saw on tv late night or even on porn when they role play. But never in a million years did she think she would be seeing some shit like this in real life.

Badrick laid both the women down. One laid on her back with her legs spread open, while the other was over her, on all fours, kissing her. Badrick had his feet placed on the floor behind the other, holding his dick, slowly sticking it in her ass. As he pumped hard, she moaned. The two women continued to kiss and caress each other as Badrick devoured her asshole. He pushed and pulled and pushed and pulled until he screamed, "I'm about to come!" You could hear some people in the audience say, "Aw damn," as if they were displeased. The women got off the bed and got on the floor, sitting like muts with their mouths open and tongues out, begging for him to come in their mouth.

"Please, me!"

"No, no. Please, Badrick, I want it."

Both began pushing each other, trying to catch the come in their mouth. He stood there with this ego energy, gazing at both women while they both licked and sucked on his hard dick until every drop was gone.

The attendant walked on stage in front of all of them, "The winner is Badrick!" he announced. The other three people continued to have sex as people started to get up out of their seats and leave. "Numbers, 356, 245, 72, 400, 2, and 12, please see me at the guest box before you leave," he announced before walking off the stage.

"He called my number. That's my number!" Tajh yelled, jumping up and down.

"Good for you. Now you can pay me back my hundred dollars," Erzulie said, getting out of her seat.

"Congratulations," the rest of the women said, following her to the exit.

Tajh followed them as well down the steps. She could hear chatter from the other people. "I was sure Tracy was gonna win this time."

It got crowded fast as other people were leaving the other theaters, exiting out. As they waited for the elevator, Tajh was excited to see what she won and most importantly how she won. She didn't even know what she was playing. "So, how does this game work?"

"It's simple: you bet to see who is gonna come first."

The ladies walked out the elevator. "Beginners luck, I guess. The box office is over there," Erzulie pointed. Tajh walked over with her card with the three numbers on it. She attempted to pull out her ID and show it.

"No, that is not necessary," the attendant stopped her. "I take it this is your first time here?" "Yes."

"Well, congratulations. Here is your twenty thousand, how would you like that? Small bills or large?"

"Large, please." She started clapping her hands jumping up and down. She turned around to see if the other ladies were still there, only to see a long line behind her.

"Here you go." He handed her a thick envelope filled with hundreds totaling twenty thousand dollars.

"Thank you," she said as she took the money.

"Come back again!" he yelled to her.

"I sure will," she said, walking away.

Chapter IV

"It's not what you look at that matters, it's what you see."

THE NEXT DAY...

"Hey babe, did you enjoy yourself with my sister and the ladies?"

"It was different, but I did win twenty thousand dollars," she said, yawning while lying in bed. "Where did you go last night? You didn't come back to the room."

"I had some business to handle, then I hung out with some friends. You hungry?"

"Yeah. I think I have a hangover, but I don't remember drinking much, just Champagne." Khori leaned over and gave her a kiss on her head. "You smell good, I don't remember you having this scent."

"It's probably just being around the fellas."

Tajh got out of bed and ran to the bathroom, falling to the floor, pushing open the toilet seat.

"Babe, you ok?" Khori yelled from the bedroom.

"Yeah, just spitting up. I feel a little sick."

"Maybe you should rest today. We were invited to breakfast by my sister, but if you're not feeling well, I can just bring you back something."

"Yeah, ok, I think I'll just sit this one out." Tajh continued to vomit in the toilet while Khori took a shower. "You sure you're gonna be ok babe?"

"Yeah, I'll be fine, go ahead and hang with your family."

Khori got dressed in the room while Tajh laid on the couch holding her stomach in a fetal position. Khori walked over and kissed her on the head. "I'll be back as soon as I can, babe," he said, walking out the door.

Tajh laid on the couch thinking about the night before, trying to remember all that she'd drunken. She wasn't no amateur and, in fact, she was always able to handle her Champagne. She had to always be aware of her surroundings. Back in the hood, the niggas would see a drunk woman as an easy pass to get ass, and the females weren't any better. They would either rob you or beat your ass. Worst case scenario, both. They always found a come up preying on the weak. Tajh definitely wasn't weak. Growing up in foster care, never knowing what it felt like to be loved or to love, all she knew was how to survive by trusting no one but herself. Foster sisters who claimed they loved her but were really jealous of her. They envied her light skin with freckles. They wanted to be in her skin. They trained to mimic her every existence. How she dressed, wore her hair, and even fucked her exes. They wanted to get treated like she did. Bamboo earrings, tennis skirts, Reebok classics, hearing bones, and anything else Tajh wanted. She knew how to play them without giving up any ass. She had respect in the streets, while her foster sisters were the epitome of being hoes with nothing to show for, but some wet pussy and swollen mouths from all the dick they were eating. Tajh wasn't over possessive about no nigga; she knew they came a dime a dozen. They would be on the next bitch with a fat ass and a little waist. But she did care about her possessions. Her clothes, her jewelry, her shoes, and purses were her life. They had more value than any man she fucked with. She caught one of her foster sisters trying on her clothes one day. Tajh picked up an iron and beat her so badly, the poor girl went into a coma. Tajh did three years in juvie. The judge was trying to charge her as an adult for attempted murder. Being that was her first offense, the judge sentenced her as a minor. When she got out, she was placed in another home.

She laid on the couch for about an hour. Reminiscing about her past had her feeling much better. She thought about that crazy ass theater and what she had seen. "Lord, Lord, Lord, I could write a book," she said, jumping off the couch, grinning to herself. She walked over towards the closet, squatting down and pulling out her suitcase, eager to count her money.

"What the fuck? Yooo, what the fuck!" she searched through her bag, pulling out her clothes. "I know I'm not trippin'. I know I put it in here." She pulled out all her suitcases, searching through them all, throwing clothes on the floor. She stood up, trying to retrace her steps. "Maybe I put it under the mattress," she said, quickly running in the bedroom and lifting up the mattress. "Fuuucckk!" she screamed. Tajh could feel her anxiety kicking in. She knew she put the money in her luggage. Khori didn't know about it because she told him moments before he left.

She walked over to her purse and grabbed her cell phone, trying to call Khori. The phone rang four times before going to his voicemail: "Hi, you've reached Khori. I'm unable to answer. Your call is important, please leave a message."

"Fuck, okay, okay... Calm down," she said to herself. She quickly threw on one of the dresses she had thrown on the floor and ran out the door. "Come on. Hurry up, stupid elevator!" She stood there watching the numbers as the elevator finally reached her floor. Not even thinking, she didn't even realize that she had left her wallet and the room key. Once the elevator reached the lobby, she quickly got off, running into another guest making them drop their belongings on the floor. She ran over to the service desk. "Hi, how can I help you?"

"Hi, umh, yes, can you page…" She stood there snapping her fingers trying to remember her name. "Gabrielle, Gabrielle please."

"I'm sorry ma'am, who?"

"Gabrielle, the on-call manager."

The service attendant stood there looking puzzled. "Who?" she replied.

"Gabrielle, you're on call manager!" Tajh yelled.

"I'm so sorry ma'am, but there is no one who works here by that name."

"Okay, well page Amancia please, it's an emergency."

"Ma'am, there is no one here by that name either. Is everything alright?"

Tajh stood there frustrated. "You know what, never mind. Can you just tell me where the breakfast buffet is, please?"

"Yes, just right down that hall to the left," she pointed.

Tajh turned around and quickly ran down the hall, looking for the buffet area. She stood in the entrance way looking at the tables, trying to see if she could see Khori through the crowd. She spotted Khori and his sister sitting at a table next to a window with an ocean view. She proceeded to walk towards them when she noticed Khori sitting across from his sister holding her hands. The conversation seemed pleasing because Khori leaned over and kissed his sister on the lips. Tajh stopped walking and stood there, watching the two share a passionate kiss.

"Tajh," Gabrielle called out her name, distracting Tajh. She turned around to see Gabrielle walking towards her. "Khori said you couldn't make it to breakfast. He said you were ill. How are you feeling?"

"I'm fine." Tajh proceeded to walk over to Khori and Erzulie's table.

"Oh, hey babe, are you feeling better?" he said, letting go of Erzulie's hand.

"Umh, yes, I need to talk to you."

"Ok," he said pushing out a chair.

"No, I need to talk to you in private."

He got up and put his arm around her waist. "What's up babe?"

"Two things, what the hell was that?"

"What was what?"

"Don't fucking play with me Khori?" she said loudly.

"Lower your fucking voice, people are staring!" he replied angrily, trying to lower his voice. He grabbed her arm tightly and escorted her out of the buffet area towards the ocean.

"I saw you, Khori."

"You saw what?"

"Why the fuck were you kissing your sister on the lips?"

"Are you kidding me right now? She is my fucking sister. That's part of our culture!"

"Oh really! You think I'm fucking stupid!"

"You're acting stupid right now! I thought you were sick."

"Don't try to manipulate me! I came down here because somebody stole my money!"

"What money?"

"The money I told you I won yesterday with your sister and her friends."

"Babe, how can that be possible? No one could have broken into our room."

"I'm fucking telling you someone stole it."

"Are you even sure you won anything? My sister said you were pretty drunk yesterday."

"Yes, I'm fucking sure!" Tajh looked through the window and saw Khori's sister and her friends getting up from the table. She walked through the doors, stopping them as they were about to leave the breakfast area. "Erzulie, please tell Khori about the money I won yesterday!"

Erzulie and her friends stood there looking at her confused. "What money?"

"The twenty grand I won from the theatre."

Khori walked over to them.

"Go ahead, tell him!" Tajh demanded.

"Hunny, I'm sorry, I don't know what you're talking about. Are you okay? Khori said you were ill from all the alcohol you drank."

"Really your gonna play this game." She turned and looked at Gabrielle and Amancia. "Oh, I see. Now I'm the crazy one, right?" Tajh pushed pass the two, knocking Amancia into one of the tables.

"Where are you going?" Khori asked, following after her. He turned around towards his sister, "I'm sorry, sis." He continued to scurry behind Tajh, grabbing her by the arm.

"I don't know what fucking games you and your sister are playing, but I'm not the fucking one or the two." She walked out the lobby, trying to flag down a taxi.

"Tajh, where are you going?"

"I'm going back to the theater where we were yesterday."

"You can't go alone, it's dangerous out here. Do you even know where you're going?"

"I'll be fine. I'm a big girl, I can handle myself." A cab pulled towards the curb and Tajh got in. Khori attempted to walk around to the other side when the taxi tried to pull off, almost hitting Khori. "Sorry sir, I didn't know you were getting in, where to?"

"I don't know. Where to, Tajh?" he sat in the back seat, looking at her.

"Take me to the abandoned theater in the city."

"Which one ma'am? There's several of them."

"All of them!"

"Really, Tajh, all of them?"

"Yes, all of them," she said, raising her voice staring back at Khori.

They spent almost two hours going from one theater to the next. "Oh, that's it over there, pull over!"

The taxi pulled up to where Tajh thought she was yesterday. She jumped out of the car looking at the building. Khori got out after her. "Don't leave," he said to the driver. She walked over to the building, pulling on the doors.

"What are you doing? This building is abandoned."

"No, it's not. This is where we were yesterday." Khori put his hand on his forehead, shaking it in disbelief.

"Sooo you and my sister and her friends came here?" he pointed.

"Yes!"

"Here?"

"Yes. I'm telling you the truth. There were homeless people sitting right here and they asked for five hundred dollars and she gave it to them, so we could get in."

Trying to comprehend, Khori repeated back what he understood. "So you're saying my sister brought you to an abandoned theater, gave a homeless man five hundred dollars, and inside you won twenty thousand dollars?" he looked at her with confusion.

"Yes, yessss! That's what I'm saying!" she yelled back.

"Baby, this makes no sense. My sister wouldn't even be in this part of town, and she would never give a stranger, let alone a homeless man, five hundred dollars."

"You know what; fuck you!"

"Maybe you just had a little too much to drink," Khori suggested.

"I already told you, I only had Champagne."

"Well, I don't know what to tell you, babe. This doesn't make sense. Let's just go back to the hotel and we will figure this out."

They both got back into the taxi. Tajh sat in the back seat just staring out the window, not saying a word. She knew she wasn't making this up. How could twenty thousand dollars just disappear? Someone knew something and she wasn't just gonna let this shit go.

They pulled back up to the hotel and Tajh got out of the car, slamming the door. Khori got out behind her, "Tajh, wait."

The taxi driver got out behind them, "Excuse me, sir, you didn't pay."

"I'm sorry, how much do I owe you?"

The driver went back to the car and checked the meter. "It's sixty even."

Khori pulled out his money and handed the driver a hundred dollars. "Keep the change."

"Thank you sir." The driver took the money and sped off.

Khori walked into the building and could hear what sounded like an argument. As he got closer to the attendant desk, he could see and hear Tajh demanding to see security cameras. "Pull them, I need to see them."

"Ma'am, I can't do that."

Khori raced over to Tajh. "Stop! What are you doing?"

"Whoever came into the room would be on the cameras."

Security came rushing over. "Is everything okay over here?"

"Yes," Khori interrupted.

"No!" Tajh yelled back. "Someone broke into my room yesterday and stole my money."

"Ma'am. I'm gonna have to ask you to calm down or you're gonna have to leave."

"Ask me to leave? Why? Why would I have to leave when I was robbed?"

"Ma'am, please calm down."

Khori interrupted, "Sir, I'm sorry. I'll handle this."

"Please do," the security officer said. The other guests were standing around with their cameras out recording Tajh.

"What the fuck are y'all looking at?" Khori snatched Tajh by the hand and began pulling her.

"Get the fuck off me!" She jerked away. Khori was embarrassed. He picked her up and put her over his shoulders and walked towards the elevator. Tajh was screaming and crying, demanding him to put her down. People were watching him handle her like she was a little girl. Right when they got by the elevator, the door opened.

He waited for the door to close before putting her down. "You're an embarrassment, and you are going home." Khori stood there breathing heavily out of breath, pointing at her. "This whole weekend was a disaster, thanks to you. You sure do know how to treat a man who introduces you to his family."

Tajh started screaming, punching Khori on his back. "I'm an embarrassment? I wonder how your family would feel if they knew you fuck men for money," she said, breathing heavily in Khori's face.

Angrily, he said back, "Well, at least my dick can bring in business deals and cash flow. You's a hood bitch who fucked for a couple hundred dollas and thought you was getting paid. My shoes cost more than that little bit of money."

Tajh was hurt by his comment. She coughed up all the spit she could and spat in his face. "Hood bitch that," she said as the elevator door opened. Khori pulled a handkerchief out his pocket and wiped the spit off his face. Tajh forgot she didn't have her hotel key. Khori walked over and unlocked the door, letting her in. Once the door opened, Tajh walked over to the mini bar and began pouring a drink.

"Pack your shit, I'm calling you a taxi. We'll talk about this when I get back." She stood there with her drink in her hand, watching Khori fix his clothes. "What!" he said while fixing his hair in the mirror.

"You still didn't explain why you were kissing your sister like that?"

He stopped what he was doing and slowly walked over to Tajh and whispered in her ear, "Maybe she isn't really my sister, or maybe she is." He turned around and walked towards the door.

"What the fuck is that supposed to mean, Khori?"

He continued to walk towards the door. "Pack your shit, you've got ten minutes," he said calmly with his back towards her. She finished drinking her drink before throwing the glass at the door. Khori looked at her in disappointment and shook his head. He picked up the hotel phone and asked the front desk to call a taxi.

Tajh sat on the bed in deep thought about everything that had happened. "Let's go, the taxi will be here any moment."

"I need to finish getting my stuff."

"I'll bring them back when I leave," Khori said calmly. He grabbed her suitcase and escorted her out the door. Once they reached the lobby, Khori walked over to the concierge while Tajh waited for him by the elevator. "Wait right here, I have to take care of something," he said. "I need to change my room, please," Khori demanded at the front desk.

"Yes sir. Is everything ok?"

"Actually, no. I'm embarrassed to say, but I'm visiting and met a young lady, and um, you know…"

"Yes, I understand, sir. Which room are you staying in?"

"205."

"Okay. Your name please?"

"Christopher Dunkin."

"Okay, Mr Dunkin. I will be more than happy to switch your room."

"Thank you."

"You are welcome, sir. Here is your new room key. You will be staying in room 506."

"Thank you madam."

"You're welcome. Enjoy."

Khori hurried up and put the new room key in his pocket before turning around. He looked to see if Tajh was paying him any attention before walking over to her. "There's a taxi outside," he said, nodding his head for her to start walking. He grabbed her bag and proceeded to the exit and she followed behind him.

"When are you coming back?" she asked, getting into the taxi.

"Two days." He closed the door and watched the taxi drive away.

"Where to ma'am?"

"The airport please." Tajh sat back, looking out the window. "How long is the drive?"

"Ummh, about an hour, give or take, depending on traffic."

"Ok, thank you."

With her head leaned against the window, she thought about Khori kissing his sister. She questioned whether she'd really seen what she thought she did. The whole him fucking another man and denying his sexuality. What were they into? Even down to them betting on who came first at a sex theater. She didn't even know such things existed. She saw a lot growing up, but this was some twisted shit. This wasn't her world or her scene. But it intrigued her, sparked her interest. If there was money to be made, she wanted in and knew she had to get with the program. Khori was right about one thing: All the shit she had to do before didn't bring in no real money. Fucking dudes for a couple hundred here and there, robbin folks, scamming old heads out they Social Security wasn't it. She was rolling with the big dawgs now. Now was not the time to have pride and ego when she was tryna get and secure a real bag. She had to put that emotional shit to the side and think logically.

Tajh grabbed her phone out of her purse and decided to text Khori to save face.

'Babe, I just wanted to say I apologize for jumping to conclusions. This is all new to me. I would like to put this behind us and move forward.'

She waited a couple of minutes to see if he read her text but it only said delivered. Assuming he was still mad at her, she gave him some time. Tajh continued to set her sights on the attractions of Jamaica to get Khori and everything off her mind. She didn't want to leave Jamaica having a bad taste in her mouth. On the ride back to the airport, she checked her phone several times to see if Khori had read her texts. But he hadn't.

"What flight ma'am?" the taxi driver asked.

"American," she replied, looking to see how busy it was as they pulled up.

He pulled over and popped the trunk. "How much is it?"

"Forty-five even ma'am," he replied.

She took three twenties out her wallet and handed it to him. "Thank you, sir."

He took the money. "How much change do you want back?"

"Just keep the whole thing."

"Thank you." He proceeded to get out of the taxi to grab her bag.

"I've got it. It's okay. Thanks." She got out, grabbed her bags, and proceeded through the airport doors.

Tajh worried that Khori wasn't going to respond. She was trying to play it cool, like she wasn't bothered. 'Hey babe, I made it back to the airport safely, just wanted to let you know just in case you were worried. I know the reception here is bad. Give me a call.'

Six hours passed and her flight landed. She couldn't check her phone because it was on airplane mode. *I'll just give him a day, he'll call,* she thought to herself. She arrived back at their house around nine thirty in the evening, tired and stressed. She threw her bag in the corner and headed straight to the shower.

THE NEXT DAY...

"Who the fuck are you!" Tajh woke up to an older White woman standing over her.

"What! Who the fuck are you and why are you in my house?" Tajh yelled back.

"Your house?" the woman also yelled back.

"Yes, my house!"

"Lady, this is my house, you got one minute to get the fuck out or I'm calling the police!" the lady screamed.

"Honey, what's going on?" a middle aged White man came walking into the room. He looked shocked seeing Tajh laying naked in the bed. "Who's this?" he turned and looked at his girlfriend with a smirk on his face. "Is this for me?" he started pulling off his shirt.

"What! No!" she said angrily, pushing him in the chest. Tajh lay there confused.

"Me and my boyfriend own this house," Tajh interrupted. The two argued back and forth until the man intervened.

"Okay, okay, calm down. Obviously, this is some sort of misunderstanding. She and I own this house."

Tajh got out of bed and walked over to the closet, pulling out a white robe.

"Is she putting on my robe?" The lady looked at her boyfriend and was pissed.

Tajh pulled out her phone. "There's definitely some confusion. I'm calling my boyfriend right now." She dialed Khori's number. "Hold on, I'm calling Khori and he will handle this."

"Sorry, this number has been disconnected…"

"Did you say Khori?"

"Yes."

"Oh boy. Okay, I see what's going on here. Honey, I'm sorry to tell you, but we rented out this property to him while we were out of town."

"What! No! I signed papers and everything to be on the deed."

"I don't know what to tell you, but we have owned this property for over five years now." "What!"

"Honey, look around you, if he lived here, where's all his pictures at? Everyone has some sort of pictures of their family and friends."

"Well, if that's the case, where are your pictures?"

The woman walked to the closet, spread open the closet doors, and pushed open the hangers hanging up to a safe in the back. She put in the numbers, opened it and pulled out photos of her and her family. "I hide these for when we rent out the house." She gave the pictures to Tajh.

Tajh sat on the bed, staring out the window in shock. "What the fuck is going on?" she said in a whisper to herself, trying to understand if she got played or if this was one of his plans to get a bag. *But why wouldn't he tell me?* she thought to herself.

"We can call you a Lyft," the lady said, trying to rush Tajh out.

"No, I'm fine, thank you," she responded in a low tone, feeling confused and disappointed.

Shaking her head, she sat there for a few minutes, trying to understand everything that had happened. *Did this muthafucka ghost me?* She got up and proceeded to get dressed. *Phone disconnected, house ain't his, car probably ain't his too.* She grinned to herself, shaking her head in disappointment.

CRIME AND CONSCIENCE

PART II

Chapter V

"The devil can offer you the most beautiful things."

What's going on? Tajh constantly thought to herself. She continued to call Khori in hopes that maybe his phone was broken or maybe there was no service. She just kept hearing the annoying voice of the operator say, "This call cannot be completed." *I know he can't be that mad,* she thought. Tajh pulled up to her house that had a for sale sign planted on the lawn. "What the fuck?" she blurted out angrily, trying to open her door before pulling over. She jumped out the car with her one bag, almost tripping and falling over the high curb; trying to read the small for sale sign posted in the grass in her front yard.

She stood there reading the sign in shock. "What the fuck!" she repeated, pulling the sign out of the grass, almost falling into the dirt. She grabbed her bag off the grass along with the sign and proceeded to the porch. She searched through her baby blue Birkin bag, looking for her keys, which was usually buried at the bottom. As soon as she found them, she tried putting her key in the lock but it wouldn't go in. She banged on the door several times, angry and frustrated. Tajh sat up against her door, pissed off thinking if she had left any of the windows or back door open. She got up off the hardwood porch, wiped the tears from her face, and gave herself a pep talk, while she walked around her house looking for an open window. "Bitch, what the fuck you crying for? It's just a misunderstanding, this is your house. And Khori, fuck him, he don't know who he fucking with. A queen never chase, I replace!" She climbed onto an old wooden crate that was left by the old owners. Trying to not fall, she carefully jumped up by the window, trying to grip the edge. It took her several tries but she was able to finally grab a hold of the ledge, pulling herself up far enough to push the window open. Once she got through the bedroom window, Tajh quickly opened the door to grab her bag and the for sale sign off the porch. She called the real estate agent whose face was plastered all over the for sale sign.

"Hi, this is Josephine."

"Hi Josephine, my name is Tajh Mason."

"Hello Tajh, what can I do for you?"

"So, I was on vacation and when I came home, there was a for sale sign on my property. I'm confused because my house isn't for sale, so why would there be a for sale sign up?"

"Can I have the address of the property please?"

"Yes. It is 1375 Milton Rd, San Antonio, Texas, 78112."

"Okay Tajh, I will look this property up and call you back."

"Okay great, thank you."

Tajh waited nervously, looking at her phone, waiting for Josephine to call back. What seemed like an hour was only ten minutes. Finally, her phone rang. "Hello."

"Hi, may I speak to Tajh please?"

"This is she."

"This is Josephine, the real estate agent. Are you able to come down to my office? I will be here until five o'clock today."

"Yes, I can. What is the address?"

"7401 Main Street. We are located on the fifth floor in the Professional Building downtown." "Yes, I am on my way." Tajh hung up quickly and drove down there.

Once you've been triggered, those old habits seem to creep back into your conscious mind. All the hard work of trying to heal from old thought patterns retract back to survival mode. Every woman for herself, not trusting a soul, and getting hers by any means necessary. The street life made her who she was, but the street life also crippled her inner child. Someone she never knew, someone that never existed. From an early age, all she knew was how to survive and fight. But when you are pushed to confront those demons, it makes you feel unbalanced, like you don't have control over your life. All those boundaries she fought to keep up, all those masks she wore, came falling off the moment she decided to put her trust in Khori.

It was obvious she figured he played the shit out of her. She smirked and thought, *Good fucking game.* Her being played wasn't the issue. Life is full of games. It was that she let her guard down and underestimated her opponent. Who would have thought a real estate immigrant from Jamaica would bring his ass all the way over to the states, put that thang on her, and take everything she worked hard for. Just the sound of her saying that to herself pissed her off even more so. Normally, she would have just called the homies to take care of it. This could have been an easy lick for them. But this was different. She had to be cautious and think strategically. She had to play and beat him at his own game. He had a team, a good team at that.

Tajh arrived at the Professional Building. Tajh was praying that Josephine hadn't left the office. She came running through the doors right before the assistant was about to lock the door. "Hi, can I help you?"

"Hi, yes. My name is Tajh. I have a meeting with Josephine," she said, trying to catch her breath. "Yes, one moment please." The assistant walked back into one of the offices. Tajh sat in a chair, still out of breath, waiting for the assistant to come back. "You can follow me please." Tajh followed the assistant back into one of the offices.

"Hi, Tajh, you can have a seat." Tajh sat in a chair across from her. "So here is the proof that you signed to have a Mr. Khori Davis as co-owner of the property, and this paper is proof of sale." She pulled out some documents and placed them on her desk for Tajh to view.

Tajh leaned over and grabbed the papers to read them. Her street smarts instantly kicked in. "You know what, I apologize. Yes, we did sell this property. I got another property that we owned confused; which account did the payment go to?"

Josephine took the papers and pointed to the account numbers, "Right here."

"Okay, great. Thank you." Tajh took a picture of the account and routing numbers, just in case Josephine wouldn't give her a copy. "Is it possible that I can have a second copy of these documents, just for my records?"

"Well, upon policy, we can only send them through snail mail."

"I thought you would say that. Okay."

"Which address would you like me to send these to?"

Tajh sat thinking for a second. She didn't have an address, hell, she didn't have anywhere to go.

"Which address did he use?"

Josephine pulled the papers closer to her to find the address Khori used. "Oh, here it is, this seems to be an address in Jamaica."

Tajh quickly took the papers out of Josephine's hand and quickly memorized the address. "Oh, yes. Okay, this is one of our homes we use as an Airbnb. Thank you," Tajh said with a smile. She quickly got up and left the office. She pulled out her phone to look up the routing number from the sale agreement. It pulled up the Bank of Jamaica. She knew she couldn't get her money back but she wanted revenge anyway. She walked to a quiet spot where she could think about her next step. She had to take her feelings out of the situation and approach her plan with caution. She didn't know too much about him or who he was working with, all she knew was that Khori had to pay.

She thought about everyone and everything she had been through. She left the hood to make better decisions for herself. But sometimes you have no choice but to go back. Never forget where you come from cause you never know when you might need to go back. In her case, it was time to go back to her old stomping grounds and make some shit shake again, but with a twist. She still had connections and decided to use her resources to get what was owed.

Tear Drop was her homie, who did twenty in the Pen for beating his woodshop teacher in the head with a hammer, trying to rob him in the ninth grade. He didn't get the name Tear Drop because he had tear drop tattoos on his face like they portray in the movies. He got his name because a single tear would roll down his face before he was about to fuck someone up. That was an indication to roll out or you were about to get your ass kicked. He was a known fighter, and while locked up, he took up boxing.

Tajh didn't know exactly how she was going to get Khori back; she just knew his ass was hers. She had to get back on the block for a while to stack her money. He had taken her for everything. So she laid low, planning, not wanting Khori to know she was looking for him. She hit the strip clubs on Fridays and Saturdays for a month. Three stacks a night came easy for her being built like a coke bottle, as they would say back in the day. She had that sex appeal that all the men crave. If she wanted, she could have gotten more off them. But that required her eating dick, with her ass up. She wasn't about that life. She had a little bit of dignity. Tajh didn't look at stripping the way other people did. She thought it was body art. Nothing but entertainment; exotic dancing was her helping men feel good about themselves. Men go through shit too, you know. They just don't talk about it. Taking her clothes off helped with their mental health. She painted pictures for men who had fetishes for the human body.

Every time she gave a lap dance, she thought about Khori and how she let him play on her feelings like she was some weak ass bitch. Listening to all his lies, thinking about all the red flags. She snapped out that shit real quick. Leave them feelings alone and get back to the muthafuckin bag.

A month passed. She was back and forth, staying in a rundown motel, so she could save money. She had everything she needed. Her fake passport, eighteen stacks, and her plan. First, she needed to find Khori's fake ass sister and her friends to get them on board, then get him to come back to the states. See one thing about a woman, if you name the right price, you get the right results. Besides, Tajh didn't think that was his sister anyway. She couldn't have been, not the way he kissed her. She had been around long enough to know sleeping cousins when she saw them. They weren't no brother and sister. That chick was definitely his bitch and she had to know where he keeps his stash. How much was Khori really worth, and if he got out on her, who else did he get out on? He had to have some serious bread since his ass was out here eating dick for deals and claimed he ain't gay, especially if he ain't never done a day in jail. In the hood, that shit is considered on the down low. You get killed for that shit.

Tajh booked her flight with her fake passport. When everything went down, she didn't want anything traced back to her. Instead of her normal Airbnb and lavish hotels, she laid low in a rundown motel that only accepted cash. She didn't want to seem like a tourist, so she blended in with the natives. No fancy name brand clothes, no big luggage, no flashy jewelry, her face wasn't beat, just her with a black curly wig on and sunglasses so no one recognized her. She had gotten a few garments to wear off one of the street vendors while passing through Downtown Kingston. She had taken a shuttle bus from the airport that stopped in the market district. It just so happened to be Grand Market day and all the street vendors were out. The streets were filled with people. You couldn't hardly walk through, clothes on the ground, vans everywhere with clothes, food and motorbikes. Just so many people. She was in the hood. Tajh decided to rent her own motorbike to get around and keep the cost down. She mapped out the bank location and the hotel where Khori claimed his family owned. She pulled up the website just to get some information about the hotel and who actually owned it. She wasn't surprised that Khori nor Erzulie's picture or names didn't pop up at all. Normally businesses would have the name and contact of the managers. But this was supposed to be a family resort; they all should have been on there. She googled Khori, thinking some information would pop up. But nothing did. She got up and walked to the window, drinking some pineapple juice she had gotten from the market. "Think, think, Tajh," she said to herself, looking at the sunset. "What was that name he said to the concierge?" She was in her head for a few minutes just staring at the sky. She took another sip of her drink. "Christopher!" she blurted out loud. She sat her drink down on the table and walked over to her bed. 'Christopher Dunkin,' she typed in the google search. But so many men popped up with that name. She began to get anxious and started to feel overwhelmed. "No, no, bitch; you can do this. There has to be another way." She began pacing the floor, talking to herself. "This is too broad, narrow it down." She sat back down and typed in. 'Christopher Dunkin, Kingston, Jamaica wanted list.' Still no results. "Duh, he is a con artist; he's got many manes," she said out loud, while typing in 'Kingston Jamaica most wanted.' "Bingo!" She started clapping in excitement. A whole bunch of pictures popped up. In fact, the website had over eighty profiles of men and women who were wanted. "Oh, I'm not about to look through all these. They're crazy as hell."

She went straight to the filter page and narrowed it down to men, but there were still too many people. She clicked on the search bar and typed in Khori, but nothing popped up. "Ok, let's try Christopher Dunkin." Still no results. She sat there just looking at her phone. "I'm sure one of his aliases gotta pop up," she murmured. 'Dunkin,' she typed in. "Boom, baby!" she said loudly,

jumping up and taking a sip of her juice.

There it was, a picture of Khori and all his aliases and a picture of him. "Hmm, no wonder they can't catch his ass, this picture must be old as fuck." She took a snapshot of his picture. Khori looked all rugged and nasty in the picture. He had a rough looking nappy mini afro. His beard looked matted. He did not look like the person that Tajh met. But that was because he was probably only doing petty theft in that wanted picture. They didn't know Khori stepped his game up and was rolling with the big dogs. "They ain't gonna find him in the hood, he's too smart for that." He blended in with the rich folks, the powerful folks, the ones who got serious clout but were not flashy with it. She knew she had to find a way to get him back to the states, she didn't know who all he had on his roster.

Khori's aliases was two pages long, along with a profile with what he was wanted for and a little bit of information of where he was last seen.

Dunkin Azan

Aliases: Christopher, Christopher Dunkin, Khori Reed, Khori Shalmon, Justin, Zack, Rob Atkins, Raymond Bey, Davis Willie, Stephon Murray

KINGSTON EAST

Offence: Shooting with intent committed on March 6, 2011, armed robbery, wire fraud, counterfeiting fraud, loan fraud, credit card fraud, embezzlement

Last known address: Bower Bank and Kingston Central

Frequents: Allman Town, Kingston

Tajh thought that since Khori was wanted, Erzulie just had to be on there too. So, she decided to look her up. But no results. Tajh finished her drink and laid it down for the night. Tomorrow was hunting season.

The next morning, Friday…

She was woken by the sounds of motorcycles and people yelling in the streets. She had forgotten it was Grand Market weekend,

Christmas in Jamaica. She watched over her balcony as the streets filled up with people walking by, shopping, congregating and enjoying their time. She overslept, had plans to leave around nine but she was jet lagged from her long flight. She had a strict plan and needed to stay on schedule. She wasn't there for fun; she was there to get to the money. She quickly wrapped her dreads up with a wig cap and threw on her curly wig, grabbed her sunglasses and her mini backpack and headed out the door. Her rented motorbike was parked on the side of the motel. She was surprised no one took it. All the vlogs she watched on YouTube about Kingston had her thinking it was too rough for her. She pulled out her phone, put in the GPS of the resort Khori claimed his family owned and sped off. Estimated arrival time, forty-five minutes.

Tajh enjoyed the scenery, riding through the back roads to the resort. She had enough time to think about what she was gonna say once she approached Erzulie. She just had to convince her that Khori wasn't any good for her. That he was money hungry and could turn on her, that she had to get him first.

She pulled up at the resort around one-fifteen. She had just enough time to find her and study her. The weather was great, not too hot. The last time she was there it was about 110 degrees outside. Very muggy, the kind of weather that made you want to lay up all day under the air conditioner. But this time, it was just right. She asked the greeter where she could park her motor scooter. She told him she was visiting a guest that stayed at the resort. Unfortunately, they didn't have a parking garage, so she had to leave the scooter with the valet.

She walked through the resort doors, looking around, careful that she wasn't spotted by Khori or any of Erzulie's fake ass friends. She walked straight through the lobby and out the exit towards the beach and dining area outside. She sat at one of the huts that served alcoholic beverages, looking out at the beach to see if she could spot Erzulie. With her back towards the barmaid, she heard a familiar voice. "Hi, welcome to the SeaSide. What can I get for you, beautiful?" Tajh was about to say nothing but when she had this blank stare on her face, the barmaid stood there just looking at her.

Tajh removed her glasses. "I would like a sex on a beach," Tajh demanded. The barmaid stood there, looking at her, hesitant to make the drink. With an arrogant tone, Tajh spoke, "What's the matter, didn't think you would see me again, sis?" She side eyed Erzulie, "Hurry up now, I don't have all day." Tajh waived her right hand a few times, gesturing her to hurry up like the old White rich ladies did to their help back in the day. Erzulie grabbed a glass from underneath the counter. Tajh watched her carefully as Erzulie made her drink. She wanted to be sure that she didn't slip her anything and get out on her again.

"So, why are you here?" Erzulie asked, while making Tajh's drink.

"You know why I'm here, bitch. Don't play with me!"

"You came back here over a measly twenty thousand?" She slammed her drink down.

"No," Tajh responded, sipping her drink.

"Then why are you here? You have money. I saw all the bank receipts."

Tajh started laughing uncontrollably. "Girl, you so funny." She continued to laugh louder and louder, drawing attention to herself.

"Stop it, please. You're making people look over here."

Tajh finished her drink before responding. "You see the money he has; I have nothing because you two took it all away from me, and now I'm here to collect."

"I don't know what you're talking about. I had nothing to do with that."

Tajh grabbed Erzulie by her hair and pulled her closer. "Bitch, you're gonna help me get my money and some."

"And if I don't?"

Tajh thought about her approach. She let her hair go. "Look, I didn't come here with no ill will towards you, I want to get him back. He took everything from me and I need your help. We can split the money fifty-fifty."

Erzulie backed away from the counter, thinking about Tajh's offer. "How do I know you won't fuck me over?"

"Oh, like you did me? I'm not you. I just want what is owed to me."

"Ok, we can talk. Meet me on the beach over there by the steps. I get off at seven."

Tajh smiled, put on her glasses, and walked away.

Chapter VI

"I saved you, so you could save me."

Crime and Conscience

It was seven o'clock on the dot. Tajh sat on the beach in a boogaloo watching the ocean's waves, waiting for Erzulie. "Pretty, ain't it?" Erzulie sat next to Tajh.

"Yes, it is. You're lucky you get to see this every night."

"Well, this view has it's pros and cons."

Tajh looked at Erzulie, "Oh really? So what are the cons of living out here?"

"Survival. You all come out here for the beaches, the ocean, and sunset, but us, we live in poverty and gotta do immoral things just to survive."

"You act like living in the States is any different. We do immoral things every day to survive, too. So, what's your story anyway? I know Khori ain't your brother. I saw how he looked at you, and how you looked at me."

Erzulie giggled, "No, he is not my biological brother but we grew up in the streets together. We looked out for each other."

"Oh, how did y'all meet?"

"When I was younger, my dad got killed and my mother overdosed in a whore house. I mean, I knew what she did to take care of me. She left one day and never came back. I was ten. I lived on the streets—started stealing to get by. One day, I was in the market, I was so hungry, I hadn't eaten in days. I ran pass one of the vendors and took some meat. He chased me down. I ran into an alley. I was so scared. He had a machete. Told me he was gonna cut my hand off for stealing. Khori and some of his friends were walking through the alley way and saw me squatting on the ground. I was so scared. They grabbed these big boulders and started throwing them at him. As soon as he turned his back, I ran. Later on that night, I was walking on the beach and ran into him again. Ever since that day, we were inseparable. Always looking out for each other. He was the first man I ever loved."

"So, what happened? Why aren't you two together, or are y'all together and you just let him do his thing? What's that all about?"

"We were at one point. Once we started learning the game and getting people for money, he changed. Money seemed to be all he wanted. He was sleeping around with different people for money; he no longer needed me. We do odd jobs every now and again but he is so arrogant. He promised me we would live a lavish life together, but I'm stuck still working, doing odd jobs while he lives rich. I was jealous that day you came, knowing I can't have him the way other women can."

"What do you mean the way other women can?"

"He had me sleep with a guy once, that was his mark. He was rich and married. He took pictures of us together and was gonna black mail him to get money. Khori got the money and I got AIDS."

"Oh damn!"

"Worst part: Khori didn't even care, he said I should have used a condom."

Tajh didn't come for no sob story, but she was starting to feel sorry for the chick—made her look at her life a lot different. She had it bad growing up, but nothing compared to this. This had her thinking how grateful she should be. "Okay enough of that, we need to get our money. Tell me everything you know about him, like where he lives, the names he uses, his connections, his banking information, everything." Tajh pulled out a pen. "It's too dark, I can't see."

"Well, we can't stay here. He might pop up or the others might see you. Here is my address, meet me here."

Tajh and Erzulie both went their separate ways. Tajh went to the valet and grabbed her scooter and Erzulie grabbed a taxi. They both pulled up around the same time. Erzulie's house looked like one of those tree houses that you see in the movie, *The Hobbit*. Very small, wooden, with trees and lots of grass surrounding it. It looked a little run down, old fashioned, but cute in its own way.

Erzulie got out of the taxi and thanked him by name. Tajh watched as she grabbed her keys and opened the door. "Come on," Erzulie nodded sideways, giving her the okay to follow her. Tajh took off her helmet and followed her through the door. She couldn't help but to browse the living room area with her eyes, scoping how she lived, making sure there was some truth to her sob story from earlier. From the looks of her house compared to how Khori was living, she was definitely telling the truth.

Erzulie offered her something to drink, "Would you like any juice, water, or vodka?"

"No, I'm fine, thank you."

"Okay, have a seat so we can talk."

Tajh sat down in a wicker chair with a blue plaid padded cushion on it. Erzulie sat on her gray couch that sank in when she sat down. Her couch was smothered with pillows of multiple textures and patterns. She grabbed one and hugged it tight to her chest while sitting

Indian style. Her house was so quiet, you could hear a pin drop. "So, what did you have in mind?" Erzulie asked, breaking the silence.

Pulling out her notepad and pen, she asked, "As I was saying earlier, where does he live?" She laughed. Tajh looked at her confused. "What's so funny?"

"Khori lives everywhere, that's how he keeps his money, that's how he never gets caught. He rents out Airbnbs. Most times he squats–"

"What's squat?" Erzulie laughed again, shaking her head. "Stop laughing. I'm serious. What is squat?"

Erzulie stopped laughing once she realized Tajh really didn't know what squatting was. "Squatting is when people live in abandoned homes or when they know the owners are out of town, they break in and stay there until they return. Sometimes, if a squatter takes care of the abandoned home, the government will let them purchase the home at a very cheap price." Tajh couldn't believe what she was hearing. She sat there with a blank stare thinking about what Khori did to her back in the States. "What exactly did he do to you?"

"He…um…made me believe that the house he was staying in was his and he had me sign some documents. He told me it was a contract for us to be business partners. It actually was me signing over my home to him."

"So, you didn't read it first, you just signed it?"

"I trusted him and I was drunk!"

Erzulie started laughing. "Oh, he got you good, sis."

Tajh yelled, "That shit ain't funny! He even wiped out my bank account. I worked hard for that shit!"

"How much did he take?"

"Fifty and sold my house for a hundred and twenty."

"I'm sorry, I truly am. So, what is your plan, how are you going to get it back?"

"We have to get him back to the States first. I have a fake real estate deal set up and then they're going to rob him, but first we gotta find him. That's where you come in. Do you have a bank account?"

"Of course I do."

"Okay, cool, cause I'll need your account numbers to wire you your share."

"And how much exactly is my share if I help you?"

"Fifty-fifty, like I said."

"No, I want sixty-forty! I'm putting my life in danger. He knows a lot of people over here. They could kill me. Plus, how do I know you and your friends won't run off with the money?"

"I won't. I promise."

"I need some type of collateral."

"Like what? I don't have anything?"

"Let me see your passport." Tajh pulled it out and handed it to her. She took a picture of it and gave it back. "First thing tomorrow, we will find him. I will tell him about the real estate deal. I just need you to give me contact names and pictures of the property to present to him. I don't want to go to him sounding like I didn't do my research."

Erzulie got up from the couch and grabbed a throw cover. "Here, take this, it gets cold at night," she gave Tajh the cover and walked to her bedroom.

Day 3…

Tajh woke up to a cracking sound and the aroma of bacon coming from the kitchen. She folded up the cover and placed it on a wooden stool sitting up against the hallway wall. "Good morning, do you like coffee?"

"No… I thought you all didn't eat pigs."

Erzulie stopped stirring the bacon. "We are Jamaicans, not Muslim, and I love bacon."

"I'm sorry, I thought I read that somewhere."

"You Americans are so lost." She shook her head and continued to stir the bacon. "Would you like some?"

"Yes, thank you."

Erzulie walked over to the table where Tajh was sitting with her iron skillet and pushed a couple of pieces with her spatula onto a plate in front of her. "Do you eat eggs?"

"Yes, I do."

She walked back to her stove and removed a pan from the oven with scrambled eggs. "Take as much as you like."

Tajh took her spoon and scooped some of the eggs out. "Thank you."

"You're welcome." Erzulie grabbed a piece of paper and pen out her drawer and sat across from Tajh. "So, tell me, who are the people with the deal?"

Tajh sat there for a bit; careful she didn't give out too much information. She didn't want her connects to get jammed up with the police. Dope Man set up the whole deal for her. His White boy, Charles Luman, owned a big ass house in San Antonio Texas. "His name is Charles Luman."

"Okay, tell me about the property."

"It's four bedrooms, four baths, 5,241 square feet."

"What's the address?"

"2511 Winding Vw, San Antonio, Texas, 78260."

"Do you have any pictures? He is gonna want to see the visuals." Tajh pulled out her phone and showed her. "Okay, send these to me so I can print them out; 770-564-2489." Tajh quickly sent the photos. "How much is he selling it for?"

"Ninety."

"Ninety? That's all?! He might question why he is selling this so cheap... Okay, I'll figure it out." Erzulie grabbed her phone and called Khori.

"Hello."

"Hey, what are you doing right now?"

"I'm sleeping, Erzulie. What do you want?"

"I have our next mark."

"Do tell.

"Where are you at? You need to see this for yourself?"

"I'll text you the address."

"Sooo… What did he say?"

"He is sending me the address for where he's at?"

Tajh got up. "Wait, wait, wait," Erzulie stopped Tajh from leaving the kitchen. "Where are you going?"

"I'm coming with you."

"You can't come! He will see you!"

"I'll follow behind on my motorbike."

Erzulie's phone buzzed. She picked it up. "He just sent it. But listen, you have to fall back and hide before we reach the house. I don't know what type of property this is or if it has cameras, ok?"

"Okay."

Erzulie texted back to Khori telling him that she got the address and would be there soon. She called a taxi. "Why don't you have a car? Why are you always in a taxi?"

"Two things: So I don't get caught and gas is too high."

They both laughed and walked outside.

Tajh followed the taxi for an hour on her motorbike before Erzulie texted her '3 min away.' She rode past the beautiful house, trying to find a wooded area to stash her bike. From the looks of it, Khori was living his best life. There was a white mini yacht that was docked about ten feet into the ocean. It read EAGLE EYE in black and green bold letters on the front of the boat. It was beautiful to her. She could see Erzulie walking over towards the yacht in the water, trying not to fall in the small current. The water must have been shallow, about three feet high. Tajh got a little closer and hid behind some trees right behind some giant boulders, trying to get a closer view. Khori helped Erzulie climb onto the deck on the back of the boat. Her dress was soaked.

"Hey beautiful, nice to see you again," he greeted her with a hug. His dark ivory skin glistened from the morning sun. His hair was different. No more dreads, he had medium size bantu knots, some dark shades, to keep the sun out of his eyes, gold chain and the brass key he always wore on it, and black bikini bottoms that showed the enormous imprint of his dick that Erzulie couldn't help but to notice.

"You look different."

"Yeah, well you know me, my look gotta match my mindset."

"And what is that?" she asked.

"Sophisticated," he laughed. "Come, let's talk business. What's this mark you talking about?" She followed Khori up the ladder onto the deck above the boat. "Have a seat," he pointed to a black, plush seat.

Erzulie sat down admiring the view. Two women were laying naked on the other side on towels. "Who are they?"

Khori looked over towards them. "Oh, just a couple of friends."

Erzulie grinned. "When did you get this?"

"Yesterday. Isn't it nice?"

"Yes, it is. How much for this beautiful boat?"

Khori got real cocky. "It's not a boat, it's a yacht, and I paid sixty for it."

"Cash?"

"Yes." He picked up his glass of scotch and sipped some.

She proceeded to tell Khori about the property, "Charles Luman has a mini mansion for sale in San Antonio Texas. Four bedrooms, four baths, 5,241 square feet. It's beautiful." She pulled out the pictures to show him.

Khori grabbed the pictures and looked through them. "This is niceeee… How much does he want?"

"A hundred thousand. I figured we can get him to sell it cheaper and resell it or swindle it from him."

He continued to look at the pictures. "How did you find this?" He threw the pictures down on the table to focus on her.

"I know people too, Khori." She started laughing.

"Of course you do, have you reached out to him yet?"

"Yes, we can leave as early as tomorrow if you'd like to go look at it."

"We? No, no. I will go. Just give me his contact and I will reach out to him."

Erzulie knew Khori would say that. He doesn't trust anyone, especially because of all the dirt he has done. He only keeps her close because she knows so much about him. "Okay, I will text you his number."

Khori got up and walked over to the two ladies lying there. He laid down with them. "Good morning ladies!" He kissed both their butts and began feeling on their bodies. Erzulie sat there for a bit watching. That made her jealous. He should be feeling on her, kissing her.

"Can I use the bathroom?"

"Yes, of course. Go down the ladder, through the room. It's on the right." Khori continued to entertain the girls like Erzulie wasn't even there.

While Khori was occupied with the two women upstairs, Erzulie took this opportunity to find his purchase papers for the yacht. "This muthafucka is selfish, he doesn't care, he never did! I did everything, everything he asked!" she cried to herself, fumbling through a drawer, looking for his sale contract. She sat on the bed trying to figure out where he could have put them. She lifted up the mattress and pulled out a yellow envelope. It was the sale contract. She quickly folded it and stuffed it in her bra. She hurried up and put the papers back in the drawer that she pulled out and left the room.

She proceeded to go back up the ladder to tell Khori she was leaving but stopped half way up. Her sight was set on one of the women riding Khori's face while the other one was sucking him off. The sound of the moans made Erzulie turn around and just leave the yacht.

Tajh was still hiding behind the tree. She could see Erzulie walking away from the boat towards the shore. "Psst, psst."

Erzulie looked over, "What are you doing here? He could have seen you. I told you to wait elsewhere," she whispered back.

"What happened? Did he believe you?" Tajh whispered.

"Yes, he did. And why are we whispering? He can't hear us, girl, come on," Erzulie grabbed Tajh's hand. "Where is your scooter?"

They walked back over to the wooden area where Tajh's scooter was stashed. "Come on, let's go back to the city. I have one more thing I need to take care of."

"Call your guy and tell him Khori will be contacting him, then give me his number, so I can text it to Khori."

Tajh called Dope Man to let him know Khori took the bait and to get everything set up. Erzulie texted Khori the contact. They both got on the scooter and drove off.

They arrived back in the city around three o'clock. "So, where are we going?"

"I've gotta make a stop. Pull over there," Erzulie pointed to an abandoned house.

"Whose house is this?"

"This is my old house when I was a kid." Erzulie got off the scooter and walked around to the back of the house to a shed. She lifted up an old rug and pulled out a key. Tajh walked in on her dusting it off.

"What's that?"

"Nothing, and you shouldn't be sneaking up on people."

"What is your problem? Your attitude has been fucked up ever since you left the yacht. Did something happen?"

Erzulie shoved past Tajh. "Nothing!"

"No. Something happened, cause you acting like a stank bitch right now!"

"I have loved him. Always kept my word. Always had his back. He doesn't care about me."

"We both know that. So, what happened?"

"He had two other women there. They were having sex right in front of me, as if I was invisible. I'm tired of feeling alone. I'm tired of feeling used. I'm tired of giving when I don't get."

"So, what's the key for?" Tajh nodded her head.

"This is my pay back. New deal."

"New deal? What do you mean?"

"I just saved you, so you can save me. Look, I didn't have to go along with this. I could have ratted you out, better yet, we both could have gotten you. New deal!"

"What's the new deal?"

"You can have the money; I don't even want it."

"So, what do you want?"

"You let me handle that. I've got my own agenda."

They both walked back to the scooter. "Where to now?"

"Well, we gotta make sure Khori actually calls him and sets everything up, soon. But in the meantime, let's have some real fun before you leave. I'll drive." Tajh got on the back of the scooter and held Erzulie's waist. "Welcome to Jamaica!" Erzulie screamed, pulling off fast. "Do you have any cute clothes for tonight?"

"No."

"Well, let's go shopping."

Erzulie took Tajh on a tour of some popular spots that the native's hang out at. Not your average tourist locations that pop up on Google or YouTube. Jamaica has some hidden areas that only the locals know about. They did stop at the market and grabbed some street clothes and shoes. Tajh expressed that she was getting hungry. "What are you in the mood for?"

"I don't know, some authentic Jamaican food."

"I know the perfect place." They both got back on the scooter and Erzulie pulled up to another wooden area that had a river running through it. There were several bamboo rafts docked on the side sitting on top of a bunch of rocks.

"Where are we going?"

"We are going into the jungle."

"I thought we were getting something to eat!"

"We are, this place is a well-kept secret. Chef John, the famous Matt Robinson, Trevor, and Patrick."

They both walked across a small wooden walkway that led them to the bamboo rafts. There was a man waiting for them at the end. "Hello ladies, are you ready for a wonderful feast?"

"Yes, thank you."

He assisted them both onto the raft. Once the ladies were on, they sat on a small bench also made out of bamboo. The man was barefoot with a long bamboo pole. He bent over and began pushing the raft into the water. He used the long bamboo stick to continue to guide the raft through the river, rotating his bamboo stick from side to side of the raft. The water was so clear, you could see the different colors of the pebbles and rocks. The further they got down the stream, the deeper the river. The fish and minos swam against the waves caused by the motion of the raft. You could hear nature so clearly. As if the trees and grass were talking to each other. It was like being in a movie. It was like the universe sent the perfect breeze every so often. They saw nature close up, not just birds, but lizards, bugs, snakes, and every other life form. Even the smell was different. It was peaceful for them. Tajh was laid back on the raft, just admiring the sky and watching the birds fly over her. Just for a minute, she felt real peace. They floated down the river in paradise.

"We are here ladies!"

They arrived at the shore. He jumped off the raft and pushed it over to the rocks. They both said thank you and walked over towards the area where a stoned fire pit was set up. Chef John greeted them both and introduced them to the rest of the cooks.

"It smells delicious, what do we have here?" There were several plants and spices laid out across a wooden table.

"We have curry goat, oxtail, ackee and saltfish, pepper shrimp, bananas and sweet potatoes." They both watched as the chef washed, chopped up the oxtail with the skin on, and seasoned them. He poured on a combination of ginger, garlic, allspice spice pimento, green garlic, chili powder and some other ingredients. He blended the ingredients into the oxtails with his hands which turned them into a dark brown color. The fire pit was already lit with wood as the heat. He then placed the oxtails in a big round steel pan and placed it over the top of the grill with a lid. The next meal he started to prepare was the curry goat. They both watched as he chopped it up with a big meat cleaver. He chopped up different veggies and mixed dry and wet spices together. Normally, he would let that marinate overnight for better taste but he didn't. The aroma of the food cooking smelled so good to them both. Tajh was definitely getting the Jamaican experience, seeing the food being prepared right in front of her. Back in the States, she would just go to one of the bodegas where they served oxtails or a Jamaican restaurant. But this was the full experience, actually seeing how everything is prepared from scratch. Trevor and Patrick finally arrived with fresh coconut. Trevor was the ackee specialist. He sat on the ground with a box and a small knife, educating Tajh about ackee and saltfish. It is the national food of Jamaica. The ackee fruit has to naturally open and ripen itself or it is poisoned. He peeled out all the seeds with his small knife. As they both waited for the food to be done cooking, Patrick cut open some coconuts for them to drink.

An hour had passed by and the food was finally ready to eat. They both sat at a table covered with a jumbo elephant ear leaf as a tablecloth. The chef served them the food in increments. The first dish was pepper shrimp. They were very big. They had to pull the shrimp apart from the shell as if they were eating jumbo crab legs. They dipped their shrimp into homemade garlic sauce and licked their lips as the sauce ran down their mouths. Tajh let out loud moans as if she was having an orgasm. To accompany the fish was a scotch bonnet pepper with freshwater crayfish. Next they did a term called pot to plate, where everything is directly served from the pot to the plate. It consisted of white rice, curry goat, oxtail stew, ackee and corned pork, saltfish, fried bananas and yams. The two ate, laughed and cried talking about their life experience. Before you knew it, the sun was setting. Erzulie packed up several plates for them and paid the chef. They got back on the raft so the guide could take them back up the river to the scooter. She tipped him as well and they pulled off.

"Do you still want to go to the club or are you tired?" Erzulie yelled through the noise of the traffic.

"I'm tired, let's go back to my room." Tajh pulled out her phone and brought up the GPS with the directions back to her room. Estimated arrival time was one hour. Tajh was extremely tired and couldn't understand how Erzulie wasn't and still had all this energy to want to still go clubbing. It took them more than an hour to get back, the streets were filled with people everywhere once they got back to the city. Erzulie told Tajh to make sure her wallet was secured in her bra so they didn't get robbed while going through the extremely slow traffic. She said most young boys will pick pocket you while sitting in traffic or just walking down the street, especially at night. They run through the cars and snatch your wallet or purse. Certain areas aren't safe for women either. Human trafficking is also a thing; they will take you, drug you up and sell you. Especially young girls; they turn them into prostitutes. Tajh made sure her wallet was stuffed tight in her bra. She watched carefully once they reached the city at everyone crowding the streets of Kingston. It was so loud, almost like being in New York without the bright lights and big billboards. They finally pulled up to Tajh's motel. She pulled her keys out of her bra and proceeded to the room. "Damn, your room is worse than mine!" Erzulie laughed.

"I was trying to lay low."

"From who?"

"From y'all."

"Girl, you won't find us in these types of areas anyway, especially Khori."

"Well, I didn't want him to spot me."

"Next time you want to play Cagney and Lacey, book a better room. I'm scared here." She laughed, looking around the rundown room distraught.

"Okay, enough about my room, let's get some rest. I'll call my connect in the morning to see if Khori reached out."

Tajh grabbed a blanket out the closet and gave it to Erzulie. "You can sleep there," she pointed at the couch up against the wall by the balcony.

"Here!" Erzulie pointed back at the couch.

"Yes."

"I hope I don't catch bed bugs." She opened the blanket and laid on the couch. Tajh put her phone on the charger and got in her bed.

Chapter VII

"How you get yours ain't for everybody."

Tajh woke up to her phone vibrating on the nightstand next to her bed. She turned on the light to see who it was. She didn't recognize the number because it wasn't saved in her phone.

It was a text: 'It's on. He is flying in tomorrow at 1pm. Be ready to meet us at the spot.'

Tajh texted back, 'Ok.'

She turned off the lamp and laid back down. The vibrating sound must have woken up Erzulie. "Who was that?" she turned over, facing Tajh.

"That was my connect. He said Khori will be flying in tomorrow at one."

"Well, I guess you better get ready to leave today then."

Tajh laid there nervous, thinking how things could possibly go wrong. She was about that life…but was she really? These men were die hard killers; people changed in jail. They were her homies but what if they got out on her. She could end up in jail or even dead. She turned the lamp back on and checked the outgoing flights from Jamaica. She had just enough money to get back. She got up and started packing her bag.

Erzulie laid there watching her. "Once the deal goes down, it's imperative that you call me." Erzulie got off the couch and proceeded to leave. 'Where are you going?"

"I have some things I need to do on my end. I'll see you soon." Erzulie left out the door.

Tajh finished packing her bag and headed down the steps to check out. When she got outside, Erzulie was getting into a taxi, Tajh waved goodbye. She called the scooter company and told them where they could pick up the scooter and left the money with the front desk of the motel along with the key. She too called a taxi to head to the airport.

Erzulie went straight to the bank where there was a safety deposit box. She pulled out a key, it looked the same as the one Khori wore around his neck. "Hello, may I help you?"

"Yes, I need access to box 101 please."

"May I see your identification please?" Erzulie pulled out her ID and showed it to the teller. She verified her name along with Khori's. "Is this a shared account?"

"Yes, it is."

"Okay, I will buzz you in."

She walked over by a door three feet from the teller and waited for her to buzz her in. Erzulie looked for box 101 and pulled out the key to open the box. The box was filled with deeds of properties from all over the world that Khori had bought or swindled from people. Erzulie took out a pen and began to sign her name on all of them. See, Khori had allowed Erzulie to have access to be on the account where he kept his deeds, but he never gave her a key to open the box. He was a master manipulator, gaining her trust and allowing her to think she was of some importance to him. He'd put her on the account, letting her believe he trusted her, but not enough to give her a copy of the key he wore around his neck. So, one day when he was drunk and asleep, she took the key and got a copy made. Those properties and the mini yacht were worth more than the money Khori kept in his bank account and Erzulie knew that. Over fifteen deeds were in that box. Deeds from Dubai, Hawaii, Jamaica, Texas, Florida, Belize, and even Thailand.

Crime and Conscience

This man was a big time real estate guru but an even bigger scammer. She took all the deeds out, folded them, and put them in her bra. She locked the box back, put it back and left.

"Did you find everything ok ma'am?"

"Yes, I did, thank you." She walked out of the bank.

Tajh arrived back in Texas and met up with Teardrop and Dope man, going over the plan to make sure everything went smoothly. They agreed to split everything right down the middle. She didn't know exactly what Khori had, but she knew he was loaded.

Once Khori touched down, he texted Charles to let him know he was in town. Charles sent a driver to pick him up from the airport. Khori didn't want to take a chance running into anybody he scammed, so he only planned on staying one night in Texas. The driver pulled up to the airport arrival terminal and got out of the car with a sign that said Khori.

"That's me!" Khori walked over towards the black Lexus with his dark sunglasses on and wearing a gray two piece pants set and white Moccasin shoes. The driver opened the passenger door to let Khori in. This wasn't nothing to Khori, he was used to lavish living and exotic cars.

"Would you like something to drink, sir?"

"What do you have?"

"Water, scotch, vodka?"

"I'll take some water."

The driver grabbed water from the small cooler he kept in the front of the car and handed it to Khori. "How was your flight, sir?"

"Ummh, it was nice."

"That's good. We will be there shortly, sir." Khori opened his water, took a sip, closed his eyes and relaxed the whole ride there. "Sir, we're here."

They pulled up to a lavish white house surrounded by palm trees with a long driveway paved with red stone. The driver got out of the car and opened Khori's door. Khori grabbed his briefcase and his small luggage and proceeded to the stone entrance. He rang the doorbell and waited for someone to answer. "Khori?" Charles asked after opening the door.

"Yes."

"Nice to meet you, come on in." He shook Khori's hand and shut the door behind him. "How was your flight?"

"Fine, thank you."

"Well, as you can see, this is a nice neighborhood. The properties are far apart, so you get some privacy. This is the living room area, very spacious, the floors are Italian white marble." Charles proceeded to take him out onto the back patio. "You see this here; all this comes with the property." The back was a big open grassy space about three square feet, big enough for a basketball court. "Let's go see the kitchen." Charles opened up the double glass doors to go back into the house when he noticed through the living room window, several cars pulling into the driveway.

"Are you expecting anyone else?"

"No, I don't have another viewing until another hour from now." Charles walked towards the living room door and opened it before the people could ring the doorbell. "Hi, can I help you?"

"Yes." One of the men pulls out a gun and puts it to Charles' head and forces him back into the house while the other two men follow behind him. "Have a seat." Khori stood there confused, wondering what was going on. "You, over there, sit down!"

Khori sat down next to Charles. "What's this about?"

Tajh came walking through the door with a laptop. "Hey Khori." Khori was stunned to see her. "Khori, you know these people?" Charles was confused.

"No…But I know her."

"Why don't you tell this man who you are and what you did?"

He was hesitant to respond. "I-I-"

Teardrop pointed the gun at Khori. "Speak louder, nigga!"

"I robbed her."

Tajh looked at Charles. "He would have done the same to you. But, I came to rescue you and get a little payback." She squatted down in front of Khori and opened her laptop.

"What do you want?" Khori was shaking uncontrollably.

"I want what you stole and some, so you are going to transfer all your money into these accounts."

"And if I don't?"

"Then you will die."

Khori started shaking his head. "Fuck, fuck, fuck!" he started yelling. "Look, I don't have your money."

"Lies."

"I don't, I swear. Please don't kill me."

"Any other time, I would have believed you. But I know for a fact that you're lying. How's the yacht coming along?"

He looked at her. "I spent the money on the yacht. I swear, I don't have it!"

Tajh got very angry and took the gun off Tear Drop and smacked Khori across the head with it. "What are the accounts?"

Khori was about to lie again. "I swear–" She took the safety off and shoved the gun into his mouth. "Okay, okay," he mumbled. She gave the gun back to Tear Drop and proceeded with the deal. She had already had his bank website opened. Khori logged into his account.

"Let me see." She grabbed the computer off him to see how much was in his account, making sure he wasn't going to try to get out on her again. There were three hundred and fifty thousand in his account. She gave the laptop back to him and read off the account numbers. "Transfer over one hundred and sixteen thousand to account number 14567888; another one hundred and sixteen to 77734522; and the last one hundred and thirteen thousand to account number 99457368." Khori did just that. Blood was dripping from his face onto the laptop. "Let me see." She took the laptop back to make sure the money was transferred over.

"It's not working."

Crime and Conscience

Charles suggested a wire transfer. Khori looked at him in anger, like, nigga what are you doing?

"Do it again; this time, what he said?" Tajh repeated the account numbers and amounts again. This time, it said pending. "What, what we gonna do, we can't wait here for this to complete."

"Wire's don't take long."

She grabbed his phone and told him to call the bank to authorize it. With the gun still on Khori, he called, trembling on the phone. "Check your account?" Dope Man pulled out his phone and the money was there. Tajh closed the laptop and called Erzulie. She could hear a phone ringing as if she was close.

"Hello?"

"Hello, it's done."

"Good." Erzulie came walking through the front door with her gun out, and shot Khori in the head.

Tajh was shocked to see her. "Yo, what the fuck! How did you get here?"

"I told you I would see you again. Plus if you wouldn't have killed Khori, he would have kept doing this. I told you he knew people in high places. He would have come after you."

"But how did you get here so fast, you don't even know them!"

"I had the address remembered. That's why I said you could keep the money." Erzulie walked over to Khori and snatched the key off his chest. "The one lesson I learned from you, that how you get yours ain't for everybody."

Printed in the USA
CPSIA information can be obtained
at www.ICGtesting.com
LVHW010104090823
754721LV00003B/320

9 781734 951189